The Tales of Miyazawa Kenji

装幀 ● 菊地信義
装画 ● 野村俊夫
挿画 ● 山口マオ

First Edition 1996

ISBN4-7700-2081-3
  00 01 15 14 13 12 11 10

ベスト・オブ
宮沢賢治短編集
The Tales of Miyazawa Kenji

宮沢賢治［著］
ジョン・ベスター［訳］

はじめに

数十年にわたり日本語を、数多くの文学作品も含めて英語に翻訳してきましたが、宮沢賢治の童話ほど訳者の私をおおいに愉しませた（そしておおいに手こずらせた）作品はそうそうありません。つまり彼の童話には、私がこれまで訳した大人向け・子ども向けのどの作品よりも真の独創性と普遍的な魅力があると、常々感じてきました。

賢治の文学の「普遍性」というのは、日本人の細々とした社会生活や個人の心理を描いていないから、外国人が読んでも親しみやすいものになっているけれども、しかしもっと積極的にいえば宮沢文学の「普遍性」は、賢治が常に登場人物の背景として、特定の国ではなく宇宙を意識しているから生じるのです。星空を背景に人間を描き、日常生活にじゃまされないようにしています。

こう言うとちょっとややこしく聞こえるかもしれませんが、賢治は同時にきわめてすぐれた具象の作家でもあります。彼の描く宇宙、―天空、自然、大地―はどれもみな、光と音と動きに満ち溢れています。そして、それら全てをそのままの姿で素直にながめているだけなのです。哲学的なごたくを大げさに並べたり、反発したり、嘆いたりはしません。もっとも彼の童話は、童話というものがいつもそうであるように読む者に常に何かを教えてくれます。ただ賢治の教え方は決して押しつけるという類のものではないのです。登場人物を見る賢治の目はやさしさに溢れていますが、その瞳に感傷の影がさすことはほとんどありません。また彼は世界をその残酷さも美しさもひっくるめ、ありのままを見ていますが、その描写が西洋の童話に時おりあるようにグロテスクになったり残酷に

4

Foreword

In several decades of translating Japanese—including many literary works—into English, few works have given me so much pleasure (and hard work) as the children's tales of Miyazawa Kenji. I have felt, in short, that they had more genuine originality, and a more universal appeal, than almost anything else I have done, irrespective of whether it was aimed at adults or children.

The "universality" is partly due of course to the simple fact that they do not deal with the day-to-day details of Japanese society and the Japanese psychology, so that they present fewer difficulties for the foreign reader. But in the more positive sense the "universality" means that Miyazawa is always aware of man against the background, not of any one country, but of the universe; he sets man against the stars, without the intervening trivia of daily life.

This may sound unnecessarily abstract, yet Miyazawa is at the same time the most concrete of writers. His universe—the heavens, nature, the earth—is full of light and sounds and movement. And he views it all just as it is, with a kind of absolute innocence and without any philosophical resentment, fist-waving or wailing. His stories always teach us something, in the manner of children's stories everywhere. Yet he teaches without imposing in any way. He views his characters with compassion, but almost never with sentimentality. His view of the world—its cruelty as well as its beauty—is clear-eyed, but he is never

なったりすることは決してありません。彼の文章は時に神秘的になったり読み手を戦慄させることはあっても、決して暗くなることはないのです。

　『銀河鉄道の夜』と『風の又三郎』のほか、この20余年の間に25の賢治の作品を英語に翻訳しました。これらの小品はすべて、1993年に出版された『Once and Forever』と題する本にまとめられています。そして本書にはこれらの作品群の中から、賢治の物語の多様さ、幅広さを示すのに適切と編集者が判断した八編を収録しました。

　あえて自分の意見を言わせてもらうと、先に挙げた二つの長編が日本では、特に若い人たちから高い人気を得ていますが、賢治の力量がいかんなく発揮されているのはむしろ他の短編のほうではないかと思うのです。実際短編の中には、構成の充実した完成度の高い作品が少なくありません。私としては、『銀河鉄道の夜』と『風の又三郎』に登場する多くのエピソードが他の短編に劣らず美しく感動的であるのはよく分かるけれども、全体として見ると——そしてこれは、翻訳者として作品を微細な点まで吟味せねばならないとなると、いっそうはっきり感じられるのですが——これらの両作品にはところどころ話の飛躍や矛盾が散見されたり、芸術的な密度にばらつきがあったりして、構成的には必ずしも完璧とはいえません。つまり両者は未完成なのです。もし賢治がもっと長く生きていたら大幅に書きかえたのではないかと思えてならないわけです。そして、この『銀河鉄道の夜』という物語に、たとえば本書の収録作品には漂わない感傷の匂いをわずかばかり嗅ぎとるのは、私だけでしょうか。

　本書に収録した八編のうち『注文の多い料理店』と『どんぐりと山猫』の二編はおそらく、西洋の伝統的な童話にもっとも近いものでしょう。ことに前者は、教訓物語に独特の語り口といい、狩人らが〈いつも自分たちが殺している動物の〉苦しみに対して鈍感なために最後にちょっとかわいそうなくらい手痛い目を見る

grotesque or sadistic in the way of some Western children's tales. His style is capable occasionally of solemnity, even horror, but it is never depressing.

In addition to *Ginga Tetsudo no Yoru* and *Kaze no Matasaburo*, I have translated, over a period of some twenty years, some 25 stories by Miyazawa. The whole of these shorter works were published in 1993 in a volume entitled *Once and Forever*. For the present volume, the editor has selected eight of these tales which give a good idea of the variety and range of Miyazawa's work.

If I may venture a personal opinion here, I feel that—in spite of the popularity of the two longer works in Japan, especially among young people, his art is seen at its best in his shorter works, many of which are formally very satisfying and show a high degree of finish. Personally, although I find many episodes in *Ginga Tetsudo no Yoru* and *Kaze no Matasaburo* as beautiful and moving as anything in the shorter tales, as a whole—and this becomes clear when, as a translator, one has to examine them in great detail—they are not so well organized, with occasional non sequiturs (hiyaku), contradictions, and variations in artistic density. In short, they are incomplete, and I can't help feeling that if he had lived longer Miyazawa would have rewritten large parts of them. Am I the only reader, too, who finds in *Ginga Tetsudo no Yoru* a touch of sentimentality of which the works in this volume, for example, are free?

Of the eight tales included here, *The Restaurant of Many Orders* and *Wildcat and the Acorns* are perhaps closest to the traditional Western children's story. The former in particular is typical of children's tales everywhere in the way it tells a story with a moral, and in the way the hunters are, with a touch of cruelty, punished in the end for their insensitivity

展開といい、世界各地の童話の典型ともいえる内容です。そして賢治らしからぬことに、この物語には、彼の大半の作品で常に変わらぬ背景をなしている自然―宇宙―の存在がほとんど認められないのです。つまり賢治独特の詩情があまり感じられないわけです。とはいえやはりこの作品は、構成的にもすぐれた佳作と言ってよいでしょう。

一方の『どんぐりと山猫』もまた、世界中どこの国の子どもでもきっと理解でき、かつ楽しめる作品でしょう。ただこちらの物語では、自然が前面に出てきます。描かれるものはみな、田舎の風景も、山も、その上にある宇宙も、すべてがみずみずしく、雄大で、光と動きとにうちふるえています。そして主人公の一郎と他の登場人物には、光に満ちた純真さがあり、そのために、一見素朴で可愛いだけのこの物語をもっと深いものにしています。

賢治の文学の幅広さは、先の二つの作品を『オッベルと象』や『毒もみのすきな署長さん』と読み比べてみれば明らかでしょう。これらの作品には、社会が登場し、また、他の二編にはない暗い色調があります。たとえば『オッベルと象』の最後でオッベルがたどる末路は、読者を心底戦慄させます（象の群れがオッベルの家のまわりをぐるぐる回り、ふりあげた鼻が塀越しにちらちら見える、その光景の恐ろしさといったらありません）。しかしここでも、自然の描写を忘れているわけではありません。そして、散々にこき使われた象が最後に救い出されるくだりには、一抹の悲しさとなぐさめさえ感じられます。これはすべてを愛情の目でみている賢治らしさと言えるでしょう。

『毒もみのすきな署長さん』はごく短いもので、一見わけの分からないものにみえるかもしれませんが、私には読めば読むほど、なにも大げさではないけれども、社会を鋭く風刺した見事な作品に思えてなりません。話の舞台はどこかとある遠い国（ヒマラヤあたりでしょうか？）だと冒頭でちゃんと具体的に描いていますが、そこで語られる寓意は、われわれのもっと身近なところに転がっています。署長さんは確かに悪党で、社会を食いものにしていますが、ある日とうとうその化けの皮を（「社会」ではなく、何も知らない子どもらの手によって！）はがされてしまいます。同時に彼は好感のもてる悪者で、荷物を積み

to suffering. It is unusual for Miyazawa, too, in that nature—the universe—that forms an ever-present background to most of his stories is almost entirely absent. In short, it lacks his characteristic poetry, but it is a good, well organized story.

Wildcat and the Acorns, too, is another tale that children in any country could surely understand and enjoy at once. But here, nature comes into its own; everything—the countryside, the hills, the universe beyond—is fresh, spacious, quivering with light and movement, and Ichiro and the other characters have a light-filled innocence that somehow makes the story much more than the simple, charming little tale it seems on the surface.

The wide range of Miyazawa's tales is seen if one compares the last two stories with *Ozbel and the Elephant* and *The Police Chief*. In these, society too enters into the picture, and there is a darker note than in the other two. The fate of Ozbel at the end of *Ozbel and the Elephant* is genuinely frightening (the trunks that are seen waving above the wall as the elephant's circle Ozbel's home is a brilliant touch of horror). Yet even here, nature is not far away, and there is a touch of sadness and solace at the end, when the much-exploited elephant is finally rescued, that is typical of Miyazawa's all-embracing compassion.

The Police Chief, very short as it is, might seem rather inconsequential, but the more I read it the more I see it as a skillful piece of social satire in miniature. The stage is carefully, and concretely, set at the beginning of the story in a vaguely distant (Himalayan?) country, but the story's moral lies closer to home. The police chief is undoubtedly a villain, who preys on society until he is finally uncovered (not by "society," but by innocent children!), but he is a likeable villain, too, who worries about an overloaded mule and a crying baby. He meets his punishment with good grace and a

過ぎたラバや泣き叫ぶ赤ん坊のことを心配したりもするのです。潔く、ふてぶてしい態度で刑にのぞむ署長さん。そして彼の最後の言葉に「すっかり感服」するまわりの人々。これらの登場人物に似たような人は、わざわざヒマラヤまで行かずとも見つかるのではないでしょうか。

　日本に暮らして久しい私は、『祭の晩』に漂う空気に無性に懐かしさを覚えます（実際にはこの作品は私が生まれるより前に書かれているのですが）。もっともアセチレンランプが使われているのを見た経験は一度もありませんが、賢治の描く祭りの全体的な雰囲気—その光景、そのにおい、その音を思い浮かべられる気がします。昨今の日本の若者はこの物語を読んでどれだけ感じるところがあるのでしょうか。主人公の少年と山男には、現在では少し時代遅れかもしれない純朴さがあり、その祭りの情景にふさわしいものになっています。その純朴さは、賢治の多くの登場人物に見い出されるものです。物語の最後で少年の祖父がちょっとだけ疑問を投げかけますが、それがなかったら、この作品は少し感傷的になっていたかもしれません。

　『鹿踊りのはじまり』は賢治の作品のまた少し違った型を示してくれます。最初は東北地方の日常生活に固く根を張っていたこの話は、だんだん幻想的になってきて、最後には一種の散文詩のようになります。こうした展開は『水仙月の四日』（本書には未収録）にも共通で、その結び方は、本書のどの作品にもまして美しく、胸を打たれます。ただ、この物語のもととなった神秘的な東北の踊りを西洋の読者に伝えられないのは、つくづく惜しまれてなりません。

　『土神ときつね』は本書の作品中もっとも完成度が高く、読む者を感動させる作品と言えるのではないでしょうか。自然描写は相変わらず素晴らしく、三人の登場者はきちんと区別されています。構成もよくできていてクライマックスにうまく導いてくれます。さらに、三者はみな悪意がなく、好感がもてるのに、それぞれの小さな欠点がもとで最後には災いがもたらされるという点で、この物語はまさに「小さな悲劇」となっています。イギリスのあ

touch of defiance. One does not need to go to the Himalayas to find his like, or the like of those around him who are "immensely impressed" by his last words.

I myself have been in Japan just long enough to find the atmosphere of *The Night of the Festival* extraordinarily nostalgic, although it was in fact written before I was born. Although I have never seen acetylene lamps used in Japan, I feel I can imagine the whole atmosphere—the sight, smells, and sounds—of that festival. I wonder how much the story means to young people in Japan nowadays? I feel, too, that both the hero and the *yamaotoko* match that atmosphere in possessing an innocence that may be old-fashioned by now and is typical of very many of Miyazawa's characters. In fact, if it were not for the skillful touch of scepticism introduced right at the end by Ryoji's grandfather, the story might seem a little sentimental.

The First Deer Dance represents yet another type of story. Starting with its roots firmly in the everyday life of Tohoku, it develops into fantasy and ends by becoming a kind of prose poem. In this, it is similar to *Suisenzuki no yokka* (not included here); in both these stories, I find the ending more beautiful and moving than almost anything else in the volume. I only wish that it were possible to explain to the Western reader the mysterious Tohoku dance that inspired the story in the first place....

As for *Earthgod and the Fox*, it is surely one of the most well-finished and moving of all the tales. The nature descriptions are wonderful as ever; the three characters are clearly defined; and the organization of the story leads skillfully to the final climax. In the sense that all three characters are well-meaning and sympathetic, yet each have minor faults that lead in the end to disaster, it is a perfect "tragedy in miniature." An English friend who read the

る友人はこの作品を読んで、私にこう語っています。「物語に登場するのは狐と土神、それに樺の木なのに、そのことを忘れ、読んでるうちに三者を本物の『人間』として受け入れるようになった」。

　私がこれまで翻訳した作家のうち、宮沢賢治の文章は—日本語としては必ずしも複雑でも難解でもないのですが—その味をうまく英語で伝えるのに苦労させられる、訳者泣かせの筆頭格です。こう言うと、賢治の文学をよくご存知の方はおそらく十中八九、方言の問題や賢治が多様するオノマトペの問題、そして英語に翻訳不可能な日本の植物や日用品の名称のことなどを思い浮かべるでしょう。現によくそういう質問を受けますし、なるほどこれらは翻訳の障害にほかなりません。完全に満足の行く解決策を見つけるのは、まず不可能といってよいでしょう。

　確かに、英語には、日本語の「ワンワン言葉」にあたる表現が（子どもが犬の吠え声を「bow wow」と言ったりするのは別にして）あまり多くありません。もっともそのかわりに、同じ状態や動作を微妙なニュアンスをこめて言い分ける語彙は非常に豊富です。ですから英語では、たとえば光は "shine"（ギラギラ輝く）もすれば "gleam"（キラリと輝く）もするし、"glow"（熱をもって輝く）もすれば "glitter"、"glisten"（ピカピカ輝く）もする、その他いろんなふうに輝いたり光ったりするのです。また、人間の体や木の枝が「揺れる」というのにも、"shake"（ぶるぶる）、"sway"（ぐらぐら）、"rock"（ゆさゆさ）、"tremble"（ぶるぶる）、"shiver"（バタバタ）、"quiver"（ひくひく）などさまざまな言い方があるのです。それから英語には "cackle"（「ペチャクチャ」—ここから "cack cack" という言い方も派生します）、"crackle"（パチパチ／パリパリ）、"giggle"（クスクス）、"waddle"（よたよた）、"toddle"（よちよち）、"ripple"（サラサラ）など、語尾が "-le" で終わる単語がたくさんありますが、これらは発生的にも日本語のワンワン言葉にかなり近いものといえます。

　方言については、その味わいの多くが翻訳の過程で失われてしまいますが、これは仕方のないことでしょう。東北弁をたとえばイギリス西部やアメリカ南部の訛りにおきかえたら、おそらく読

story told me that though the chief characters are a fox, an earthgod, and a birch tree, he forgot about that and, as he read, came to accept them as real "people."

Of all the writers I have translated, Miyazawa's style is—though not necessarily complex or difficult as Japanese—one of the most difficult to render successfully in English. When I say that, the reader who knows Miyazawa well will almost certainly think of question such as dialect, the onomatopoeic words that Miyazawa uses so frequently, untranslatable names of Japanese plants and everyday objects, and so on. I am often asked about these, and they are, of course, obstacles: a completely satisfactory solution is impossible in most cases.

Certainly, English does not have many words (except for specifically children's words such as "bow-wow" for dog) of the *wan-wan* type. What it does have, however, is a very rich vocabulary of words indicating subtle nuances of the same state or action. Thus light, for example, may shine, gleam, glow, glitter, glisten, etc. etc. Human bodies or trees may shake, sway, rock, tremble, shiver, quiver, and so on. The many English words ending in "-le," such as cackle (to go "cack-cack"), crackle, giggle, waddle, toddle, ripple, etc. etc. are in fact very similar in origin to the Japanese *wan-wan* words.

Where dialect is concerned, much is lost in translation, but this is unavoidable. To translate Tohoku-ben into the dialect of, for example, the West of England, or the deep South of the United States would be to evoke sets of associations that would be remote from the Japanese countryside and spoil the atmosphere of the story entirely. In some cases, where I have felt that a "dialect" of some kind was absolutely necessary, I have invented one of my own, made up probably of fragmentary recollections of various real

者の頭にはイギリス西部なりアメリカ南部なりがいやでも連想され、賢治が描いた日本の片田舎の情景からは遠く隔たることになります。そうなれば作品の雰囲気は大きく損なわれてしまいます。とはいえ場合によってはどうしても何かの「方言」を使いたいところもあって、そうした箇所には、いわゆる、自家製の方言（あちらこちらの方言の断片的な記憶）を作ることにしました。『鹿踊りのはじまり』ではこういうやり方をしましたが、物語の終わりで重要な歌を詠む場面では、標準語に戻すようにしました。その他の場合でも、登場人物の喋り方に田舎臭くてあまり教養のない（たとえば山猫の葉書の文面のように）印象だけでも匂わすようにしました。特定の地域を想起させることがないように…。

　日本固有の事物をどう訳すかというのも困った問題で、植物や食べ物、日用品のあれこれなど、悩みの種をあげるときりがありません。これについては全面的姿勢として、こむずかしい学術用語を使ったり日本語をイタリックで用いたりというのは極力避け、前後の文脈から内容を補えるような言葉を選んで、原文の感触をできるだけくずさずに伝えることをめざしました。

　ひとつ具体的な例を挙げましょう。それは今でも胸に引っかかっているのですが、日本語の「すすき」の訳し方です。「すすき」と「パンパスグラス」が同一の植物でないことはもちろん承知しています。しかし、「すすき」の訳語を辞書で引いて出てくるのはラテン語による学名と、あとは二、三の英語名だけなのです。それも、英語を母国語とする私がかつて一度も耳にしたことがなく、いかなる視覚的イメージも呼び起こさないものばかりなのです。しかしながら、「すすき」は賢治の童話世界で（たとえば『鹿踊りのはじまり』に見られるように）極めて重要な役割を果たしており、究極の選択としてこの「pampas grass」をあえて訳語に選びました。少なくとも「pampas grass」といえば、英語の読者にもだいたいのイメージは伝わりますし、読んでいるうちに、そのイメージが読者のなかで、賢治の意図していたものに徐々に近づいていくはずです。

　さらにもうひとつ留意すべき点は、日本語と英語が全く性格の違う言葉であるということです。子どもらしい無邪気な雰囲気を醸

dialects. I did this in *The First Deer Dance*, though I allowed the deer to lapse into standard speech for their important song at the end. In other cases, I've tried at least to create the impression that the character speaking is a countryman, or not well-educated (in Wildcat's postcards, for example), without suggesting any specific area…

As for uniquely Japanese things—plants, foods, articles of everyday use, etc.—there is no end to the list of problems. My general aim is to avoid both pedantry and the use of Japanese words in italics, and to try to convey as much as possible of the feeling of the original by the choice of words supplemented by the context in which they occur.

One concrete case that still bothers me rather is the word *susuki*. I know, of course, that *susuki* and "pampas grass" are not the same. But, as translations of *susuki*, the dictionaries offer only the Latin academic name and two or three English names that I at least, as a British reader, had never heard of and that convey no visual image to me at all. However, *susuki* (for example, in *The First Deer Dance*) is such an essential element of the Miyazawa world that in the end I chose "pampas grass," since it least conveys a rough image that will be modified in the reader's mind, as he reads, into something close to what Miyazawa intended.

Another point to remember is that Japanese and English are utterly different languages. Thus the ways of creating a childlike, innocent effect, differ considerably. This is partly a matter of vocabulary. For example, to convey the correct nuance of what seems to be a simple Japanese word, it is sometimes necessary to use a "difficult" word (difficult, at least, if one looks up the "direct" translation in an English-Japanese dictionary). But in fact it is often permissible to use such "difficult" words in an English children's story; what is taboo, rather, is stiffness—the sentences, as in

し出すにしても、日本語と英語ではとるべき手法が大きく違ってきます。これは一部には語彙の問題でもあります。たとえば、やさしそうな日本語でも、その正確なニュアンスを英語で伝えるには時として「難しい」言葉を—少なくとも辞書を開いて「直接的な」訳語を探したかぎりでは難しい—使うことが必要になります。しかも実際、そうした「難しい」言葉を使うことは、英語の童話ではよくあることです。いけないとされるのはむしろ、文章が硬くなることです。日本語でも同じように、物語の文章は読者に気軽に、親しみやすく語りかけてくるように流れて行かなければなりません。

　翻訳にあたっては、原文にできるだけ忠実であるよう心がけ（言うまでもなく、四角四面な逐語訳ということではありません）、勝手に削らないようにしています。とはいってもこれは文芸作品ですし、ことに賢治の場合は、言葉の流れや雰囲気がたいへん重要な意味をもちますので、場合によっては長々しい説明口調を避けるため原文をわずかに離れたり、原文をそのまま英語に置き換えると文学的効果が台無しになるようなときは言葉を多少削除することも必要になるわけです。他方、翻訳者であるからには、所詮完全な翻訳はありえないと分かっていても、母国語の特性を生かして翻訳を補う努力をしなければなりません。

　たとえば英語は、こと音声面・リズム面に関しては非常に豊かな言語ですから、頭韻を踏むなどの工夫をほどこすことで、原文の持ち味を殺すことなく、翻訳の際に生じた穴をある程度埋めることができます。こうしたテクニックがことに重要になるのは、たとえば『土神ときつね』や『鹿踊りのはじまり』の結びの数節で、これらの箇所の翻訳にはとりわけ心血を注ぎました。原文の感じがうまく出せたかどうか、訳文は必ず頭の中で口ずさんでチェックするようにしています。

　本書は対訳本ではありますが、教科書ではありません。翻訳上の誤りやひとりよがりな解釈がありましたら、もちろんそれは私の責任です。ただ自分の希望としては読者の皆さんには、誤訳に気を取られるよりも、訳文を（できるなら声を出して）読んで、賢治の童話が別の言語ではどのように聞こえるのかを味わっていただきたい。英

the Japanese too, must flow, addressing the reader in a familiar, relaxed way.

In translating, I believe in the greatest possible faithfulness to the original—which is not to say, necessarily, dictionary equivalents; and in not cutting. Even so, this is literature, and with Miyazawa in particular the flow of the language, the atmosphere, are all-important. Occasionally, it is necessary to be slightly free, to avoid the pedantic solution, even to cut a few words if to translate them would spoil a literary effect. On the other hand the translator, while recognizing that a translation cannot be perfect, must try to compensate for this by taking advantage of the special features of his own language.

English, for example, is a particularly rich language phonetically and rhythmically, so it is possible to add some effects (e.g. alliteration) that make up for the deficiencies of the translation without violating the spirit of the original. This is particularly important, for example, in the concluding passages of stories such as *Earthgod and the Fox* or *The First Deer Dance*. I devoted particular attention to such passages. Whether I succeeded or not, I always test my own translations by reading them aloud in my mind.

Although this is a bilingual edition, it is not a textbook. I accept responsibility of course for my mistakes and arbitrary decisions. But, for myself, I would rather the reader concentrate, not so much on searching for errors as on reading the stories (possible, even, aloud to himself) to see how Miyazawa sounds in another language, referring to the Japanese whenever he is not sure of the sense and pondering on the differences between the two languages. And if, because of the existence of this book, he reads again stories he has not seen since his childhood, or even makes

語の意味が不明瞭なところがあればいつでも日本語と照らしあわせて、二つの言語の性格の違いをしばし考えていただきたい。そしてもし本書を手にした読者が、子どものころ読んだきりになっていた作品を再び読み返したり、初めての作品をひもをといて賢治の芸術のすばらしさを改めて体感するきっかけを得たのなら、それだけでこの本が世に出た意味は十分にあったといえるでしょう。

ジョン・ベスター

acquaintance with stories he has never read before, and realizes afresh the splendidness of Miyazawa's art, then its existence will be fully justified.

John Bester

目次

Contents

どんぐりと山猫

　おかしなはがきが、ある土曜日の夕がた、一郎のうち
にきました。

　　かねた一郎さま　　九月十九日
　　あなたは、ごきげんよろしいほで、けっこです。
　　あした、めんどなさいばんしますから、おいでん
　　なさい。とびどぐもたないでくなさい。

　　　　　　　　　　　　　　　　　　山ねこ　拝

　んなのです。字はまるでへたで、墨もがさがさし
て指につくくらいでした。けれども一郎はうれし
くてうれしくてたまりませんでした。はがきをそっと学
校のかばんにしまって、うちじゅうとんだりはねたりし
ました。
　ね床にもぐってからも、山猫のにゃあとした顔や、そ
のめんどうだという裁判のけしきなどを考えて、おそく
までねむりませんでした。
　けれども、一郎が眼をさましたときは、もうすっかり
明るくなっていました。おもてにでてみると、まわりの
山は、みんなたったいまできたばかりのようにうるうる
もりあがって、まっ青なそらのしたにならんでいました。

Wildcat and the Acorns

One Saturday evening, a most peculiar postcard arrived at Ichiro's house. This is what it said:

<blockquote>

September 19

Mr. Ichiro Kaneta:

Pleased to know as how you're well. Tomorrow I've got a difficult case to judge, so please come. Please don't bring no firearms.

Yours respectfully,
Wildcat

</blockquote>

That was all. The writing was terrible, and the ink so blobby it almost stuck to his fingers. But Ichiro was quite delighted. He put the card in his satchel when no one was looking to take it to school, and bounced up and down all over the house with joy.

Even after he'd crept into bed that night, he still kept imagining Wildcat's face with its cat's grin, and the scene at tomorrow's trial, and so many other things that he couldn't get to sleep until quite late.

When he awoke, though, it was already broad daylight. He went outside, and there were the hills lined up beneath a bright blue sky, rising as fresh and clean as though they'd just been made. He hurried through his

一郎はいそいでごはんをたべて、ひとり谷川に沿ったこみちを、かみの方へのぼって行きました。

　すきとおった風がざあっと吹くと、栗の木はばらばらと実をおとしました。一郎は栗の木をみあげて、
「栗の木、栗の木、やまねこがここを通らなかったかい。」
とききました。栗の木はちょっとしずかになって、
「やまねこなら、けさはやく、馬車でひがしの方へ飛んで行きましたよ。」と答えました。
「東ならぼくのいく方だねえ、おかしいな、とにかくもっといってみよう。栗の木ありがとう。」

　栗の木はだまってまた実をばらばらとおとしました。

　一郎がすこし行きますと、そこはもう笛ふきの滝でした。笛ふきの滝というのは、まっ白な岩の崖のなかほどに、小さな穴があいていて、そこから水が笛のように鳴って飛び出し、すぐ滝になって、ごうごう谷におちているのをいうのでした。

　一郎は滝に向いて叫びました。
「おいおい、笛ふき、やまねこがここを通らなかったかい。」
　滝がぴーぴー答えました。
「やまねこは、さっき、馬車で西の方へ飛んで行きましたよ。」
「おかしいな、西ならぼくのうちの方だ。けれども、まあも少し行ってみよう。ふえふき、ありがとう。」
　滝はまたもとのように笛を吹きつづけました。

　一郎がまたすこし行きますと、一本のぶなの木のしたに、たくさんの白いきのこが、どってこどってこどってこと、変な楽隊をやっていました。

　一郎はからだをかがめて、
「おい、きのこ、やまねこが、ここを通らなかったかい。」
とききました。するときのこは、
「やまねこなら、けさはやく、馬車で南の方へ飛んで行

breakfast and set off alone up the path by the stream in the valley. There was a fresh, clear morning breeze, and at each puff the chestnut trees showered their nuts in all directions. Ichiro looked up at them.

"Hello there, Chestnut Trees," he called. "Did Wildcat pass this way?"

And the trees paused a while in their rustling and replied, "Wild cat? Yes, he rushed past in a carriage early this morning, going to the east."

"The east? That's the direction I'm heading in. How strange! At any rate, I'll keep going this way and see. Thank you, Chestnut Trees."

The chestnut trees made no answer but went on scattering their nuts around. So Ichiro went a little farther, and came to the Flute Falls. About halfway up a pure white cliff, there was a small hole through which the water spurted, whistling like a flute before dropping with a roar into the valley below. Facing the waterfall, Ichiro shouted up at it:

"Hello there, Flute Falls. Did Wildcat pass this way?"

"Wildcat?" came a high, whistly voice. "Yes, he rushed past in a carriage a while ago, going to the west."

"The west?" said Ichiro. "That's where my home is. How strange! Anyway, I'll go a bit farther and see. Thank you, Waterfall."

But the waterfall was already whistling to itself as it always did. So Ichiro went on a bit and came to a beech tree. Under the tree, a crowd of white mushrooms were playing together in a funny kind, of orchestra: *tiddley-tum-tum*, *tiddley-tum-tum*. Ichiro bent down toward them.

"Hello, Mushrooms," he said. "Did Wildcat pass this way?"

きましたよ。」とこたえました。一郎は首をひねりました。

「みなみならあっちの山のなかだ。おかしいな。まあもすこし行ってみよう。きのこ、ありがとう。」

きのこはみんないそがしそうに、どってこどってこと、あのへんな楽隊をつづけました。

一郎はまたすこし行きました。すると一本のくるみの木の梢（こずえ）を、栗鼠（りす）がぴょんととんでいました。一郎はすぐ手まねぎしてそれをとめて、

「おい、りす、やまねこがここを通らなかったかい。」とたずねました。するとりすは、木の上から、額（ひたい）に手をかざして、一郎を見ながらこたえました。

「やまねこなら、けさまだくらいうちに馬車でみなみの方へ飛んで行きましたよ。」

「みなみへ行ったなんて、二（ふた）とこでそんなことを言うのはおかしいなあ。けれどもまあもすこし行ってみよう。りす、ありがとう。」りすはもう居ませんでした。ただくるみのいちばん上の枝がゆれ、となりのぶなの葉がちらっとひかっただけでした。

一郎がすこし行きましたら、谷川にそったみちは、もう細くなって消えてしまいました。そして谷川の南の、まっ黒な榧（かや）の木の森の方へ、あたらしいちいさなみちがついていました。一郎はそのみちをのぼって行きました。榧の枝はまっくろに重なりあって、青ぞらは一きれも見えず、みちは大へん急な坂になりました。一郎が顔をまっかにして、汗をぽとぽとおとしながら、その坂をのぼりますと、にわかにぱっと明るくなって、眼がちくっとしました。そこはうつくしい黄金（きん）いろの草地で、草は風にざわざわ鳴り、まわりは立派なオリーヴいろのかやの木のもりでかこまれてありました。

その草地のまん中に、せいの低いおかしな形の男が、膝（ひざ）を

"Wildcat?" replied the mushrooms. "Yes, he rushed past in a carriage early this morning, going to the south."

"That's strange," said Ichiro, in growing puzzlement. "That's in those mountains over there. Anyway, I'll go a bit farther and see. Thank you, Mushrooms."

But the mushrooms were already busy again, playing their peculiar music, *tiddley-tum-tum, tiddley-tum-tum....*

Ichiro was walking on when he noticed a squirrel hopping about in the branches of a walnut tree.

"Hey, Squirrel!" called Ichiro, waving at him to stop. "Did Wildcat pass this way?"

"Wildcat?" said the squirrel, shading his eyes with a paw as he peered down at Ichiro. "Yes, he rushed past this morning in a carriage while it was still dark, going to the south."

"The south?" said Ichiro. "That's strange—that's twice I've been told that. Ah well, I'll go a bit farther and see. Thank you, Squirrel."

But the squirrel had gone. All he could see was the topmost branches of the walnut tree swaying a little, and the leaves of the neighboring beech tree flashing for a moment in the sun.

A little farther on and the path along the stream grew narrower, then disappeared altogether. There was another narrow path, however, leading up toward the dark wood to the south of the stream, so Ichiro set of up it. The branches of the trees were heavy and so close together that not the tiniest patch of blue sky was to be seen. The path became steeper and steeper. Ichiro's face turned bright red, and sweat fell off it in great drops. But then, quite suddenly, he came out into the light. He had reached a beautiful golden meadow. The grass rustled in

曲げて手に革鞭をもって、だまってこっちをみていたのです。

　一郎はだんだんそばへ行って、びっくりして立ちどまってしまいました。その男は、片眼で、見えない方の眼は、白くびくびくうごき、上着のような半纏のようなへんなものを着て、だいいち足が、ひどくまがって山羊のよう、ことにそのあしさきときたら、ごはんをもるへらのかたちだったのです。一郎は気味が悪かったのですが、なるべく落ちついてたずねました。

「あなたは山猫をしりませんか。」

　するとその男は、横目で一郎の顔を見て、口をまげてにやっとわらって言いました。

「山ねこさまはいますぐに、ここに戻ってお出やるよ。おまえは一郎さんだな。」

　一郎はぎょっとして、一あしうしろにさがって、

「え、ぼく一郎です。けれども、どうしてそれを知ってますか。」と言いました。するとその奇体な男はいよいよにやにやしてしまいました。

「そんだら、はがき見だべ。」

「見ました。それで来たんです。」

「あのぶんしょうは、ずいぶん下手だべ。」と男は下をむいてかなしそうに言いました。一郎はきのどくになって、

「さあ、なかなか、ぶんしょうがうまいようでしたよ。」と言いますと、男はよろこんで、息をはあはあして、耳のあたりまでまっ赤になり、きもののえりをひろげて、風をからだに入れながら、

「あの字もなかなかうまいか。」とききました。一郎は、おもわず笑いだしながら、へんじしました。

「うまいですね。五年生だってあのくらいには書けないでしょう。」

the breeze, and all around stood fine, olive-colored trees.

There, in the middle of the meadow, a most odd-looking little man was watching Ichiro. His back was bent, and in his hand he held a leather whip. Ichiro slowly went nearer, then stopped in astonishment. The little man was one-eyed, and his blind eye, which was white, was moving nervously all the time. He wore a funny kind of workman's jacket. His legs were very bandy, like a goat's, and—most peculiar of all—his feet were shaped like spades.

"You wouldn't happen to know Wildcat, would you?" Ichiro asked, trying not to show his nervousness.

The little man looked at Ichiro with his one eye, and his mouth twisted in a leer.

"Mr. Wildcat will be back in just a moment," he said. "You'll be Ichiro, I suppose?"

Ichiro started back in astonishment.

"Yes, I'm Ichiro," he replied. "But how did you know?"

The strange little man gave an even broader leer.

"Then you got the postcard?" he asked.

"Yes, that's why I came," Ichiro said.

"Badly written, wasn't it?" asked the little man, looking gloomily down at the ground. Ichiro felt sorry for him.

"No," he said. "It seemed very good to me."

The man gave a little gasp of joy and blushed to the tips of his ears. He pulled his coat open at the neck to cool himself, and asked:

"Was the handwriting all right?"

Ichiro couldn't help smiling.

"It was fine," he said. "I doubt if even a fifth grader could write that well."

すると男は、急にまたいやな顔をしました。
「五年生っていうのは、尋常五年生だべ。」その声が、あんまり力なくあわれに聞こえましたので、一郎はあわてて言いました。
「いいえ、大学校の五年生ですよ。」
　すると、男はまたよろこんで、まるで、顔じゅう口のようにして、にたにたにたにた笑って叫びました。
「あのはがきはわしが書いたのだよ。」
　一郎はおかしいのをこらえて、
「ぜんたいあなたはなにですか。」とたずねますと、男は急にまじめになって、
「わしは山ねこさまの馬車別当だよ。」と言いました。
　そのとき、風がどうと吹いてきて、草はいちめん波だち、別当は、急にていねいなおじぎをしました。
　一郎はおかしいとおもって、ふりかえって見ますと、そこに山猫が、黄いろな陣羽織のようなものを着て、緑いろの眼をまん円にして立っていました。やっぱり山猫の耳は、立って尖っているなと、一郎がおもいましたら、山猫はぴょこっとおじぎをしました。一郎もていねいに挨拶しました。
「いや、こんにちは、きのうははがきをありがとう。」
　山猫はひげをぴんとひっぱって、腹をつき出して言いました。
「こんにちは、よくいらっしゃいました。じつはおとといから、めんどうなあらそいがおこって、ちょっと裁判にこまりましたので、あなたのお考えを、うかがいたいとおもいましたのです。まあ、ゆっくり、おやすみください。じき、どんぐりどもがまいりましょう。どうもまい年、この裁判でくるしみます。」山猫は、ふところから、巻き煙草の箱を出して、じぶんが一本くわえ、

The little man suddenly looked depressed again.

"When you say fifth grader, you mean at primary school, I suppose?" His voice was so listless and pathetic that Ichiro was alarmed.

"Oh, no," he said hastily. "At university."

The little man cheered up again and grinned so broadly that his face seemed to be all mouth.

"*I* wrote that postcard," he shouted.

"Just who are you, then?" asked Ichiro, trying not to smile.

"I am Mr. Wildcat's coachman!" he replied.

A sudden gust of wind rippled over the grass, and the coachman gave a deep bow. Puzzled, Ichiro turned around, and there was Wildcat, standing behind him. He wore a fine coat of yellow brocade, and his green eyes as he stared at Ichiro were perfectly round. Ichiro barely had time to note that his ears were pointed and stuck up just like an ordinary cat's, before Wildcat gave a stiff little bow.

"Oh, good morning," said Ichiro politely, bowing in return. "Thank you for the postcard."

"Good morning," said Wildcat, pulling his whiskers out stiff and sticking out his belly. "I'm pleased to see you. The fact is, a most troublesome dispute arose the day before yesterday, and I don't quite know how to settle it, so I thought I might ask your opinion. But anyway, make yourself at home, won't you? The acorns should be here any moment now. Really, you know, I have a lot of trouble with this trial every year."

He took a cigarette case from inside his coat and put a cigarette in his mouth.

"Won't you have one?" he asked, offering the case to Ichiro.

「いかがですか。」と一郎に出しました。一郎はびっくりして、

「いいえ。」と言いましたら、山猫はおうようにわらって、

「ふふん、まだお若いから。」と言いながら、マッチをしゅっと擦って、わざと顔をしかめて、青いけむりをふうと吐きました。山猫の馬車別当は、気を付けの姿勢で、しゃんと立っていましたが、いかにも、たばこのほしいのをむりにこらえているらしく、なみだをぽろぽろこぼしました。

　そのとき、一郎は、足もとでパチパチ塩のはぜるような、音をききました。びっくりして屈んで見ますと、草のなかに、あっちにもこっちにも、黄金いろの円いものが、ぴかぴかひかっているのでした。よくみると、みんなそれは赤いずぼんをはいたどんぐりで、もうその数ときたら、三百でも利かないようでした。わあわあわあわあ、みんななにか言っているのです。

「あ、来たな。蟻のようにやってくる。おい、さあ、早くベルを鳴らせ。今日はそこが日当たりがいいから、そこのとこの草を刈れ。」山猫は巻きたばこを投げすてて、大いそぎで馬車別当にいいつけました。馬車別当もたいへんあわてて、腰から大きな鎌をとりだして、ざっくざっくと、やまねこの前のとこの草を刈りました。そこへ四方の草のなかから、どんぐりどもが、ぎらぎらひかって、飛び出して、わあわあわあわあ言いました。

　馬車別当が、こんどは鈴をがらんがらんがらんがらんと振りました。音はかやの森に、がらんがらんがらんがらんとひびき、黄金のどんぐりどもは、すこししずかになりました。見ると山猫は、もういつか、黒い長い繻子の服を着て、勿体らしく、どんぐりどもの前にすわっていました。まるで奈良のだいぶつさまにさんけいするみ

"Oh, no thank you," said Ichiro, startled.

"Ho-ho! Of course, you're still too young," said Wildcat with a lordly kind of laugh. He struck a match and, screwing up his face self-consciously, puffed out a cloud of blue smoke. His coachman, who was stiffly standing by awaiting orders, seemed to be dying for a cigarette himself, as there were big tears rolling down his face.

Just then, Ichiro heard a tiny crackling sound at his feet, like salt being tossed on a fire. He bent down in surprise to look and saw that the ground was covered with little round gold things, glinting in the grass. He looked closer and found that they were acorns—there must have been over three hundred of them—all wearing red trousers and all chattering away about something at the top of their voices.

"Here they come. Just like a lot of ants," said Wildcat, throwing away his cigarette. Hurriedly he gave orders to the coachman. "You there, ring the bell," he said. "And cut the grass just here, where it's sunny."

The coachman took up a big sickle at his side and swished down the grass in front of Wildcat. Immediately, the acorns came rushing out from the surrounding grass, glittering in the sun as they came, and chattering like mad.

The coachman rang his bell. *Clang, clang!* it went. *Clang, clang!* the sound echoed through the woods, and the golden acorns became a little quieter. Unnoticed by Ichiro, Wildcat had put on a long black satin gown and was now sitting there in front of them, looking important. It reminded Ichiro of pictures he had seen of crowds of tiny worshipers before a great bronze idol.

んなの絵のようだと一郎はおもいました。別当がこんど
は、革鞭を二三べん、ひゅうぱちっ、ひゅう、ぱちっと
鳴らしました。

　空が青くすみわたり、どんぐりはぴかぴかしてじつに
きれいでした。

「裁判ももう今日で三日目だぞ、いい加減になかなおりをし
たらどうだ。」山猫が、すこし心配そうに、それでもむりに
威張って言いますと、どんぐりどもは口々に叫びました。

「いえいえ、だめです、なんといったって頭のとがって
るのがいちばんえらいんです。そしてわたしがいちばん
とがっています。」

「いいえ、ちがいます。まるいのがえらいのです。いち
ばんまるいのはわたしです。」

「大きなことだよ。大きなのがいちばんえらいんだよ。
わたしがいちばん大きいからわたしがえらいんだよ。」

「そうでないよ。わたしのほうがよほど大きいと、きの
うも判事さんがおっしゃったじゃないか。」

「だめだい、そんなこと。せいの高いのだよ。せいの高
いことなんだよ。」

「押しっこのえらいひとだよ。押しっこをしてきめるん
だよ。」もうみんな、がやがやがやがや言って、なにが
なんだか、まるで蜂の巣をつっついたようで、わけがわ
からなくなりました。そこでやまねこが叫びました。

「やかましい。ここをなんとこころえる。しずまれ、し
ずまれ。」

　別当がむちをひゅうぱちっとならしましたのでどんぐ
りどもは、やっとしずまりました。山猫は、ぴんとひげ
をひねって言いました。

「裁判ももうきょうで三日目だぞ、いい加減に仲なおり
したらどうだ。」

Swish, crack! swish, crack! went the coachman with his whip. The sky was blue and cloudless, and the acorns sparkled beautifully.

"Let me remind you, this is the third day this case has been going on." Wildcat began. "Now, why don't you call it off and make it up with each other?"

His voice was a little nervous, but he forced himself to sound important. No sooner had he spoken, though, than the acorns set up a commotion again.

"No, that's impossible! Whatever you say, the one with the most pointed head is best. And it's me who's the most pointed."

"No, you're wrong, the roundest one's best. I'm the roundest!"

"It's size, I tell you! The biggest. I'm the biggest, so I'm the best!"

"That's nonsense! I'm much bigger. Don't you remember the judge said so yesterday?"

"You're all wrong! It's the one who's the tallest. The tallest one, I tell you!"

"No, it's the one who's best at pushing and shoving. That's what settles it!"

The acorns were making such a racket that in the end you had absolutely no idea what it was all about. It was like stirring up a hornet's nest.

"That's enough!" Wildcat bawled. "Where do you think you are? Silence! Silence!"

Swish, crack! went the coachman's whip, and at last the acorns were quiet.

"Let me remind you again, this is the third day this trial has been going on," Wildcat declared, twisting his whiskers till they stood on end. "How about calling it off now and making things up?"

すると、もう、どんぐりどもが、くちぐちに言いました。
「いえいえ、だめです。なんといったって、頭のとがっているのがいちばんえらいのです。」
「いいえ、ちがいます。まるいのがえらいのです。」
「そうでないよ。大きなことだよ。」がやがやがやがや、もうなにがなんだかわからなくなりました。山猫が叫びました。
「だまれ、やかましい。ここをなんと心得る。しずまれしずまれ。」別当が、むちをひゅうぱちっと鳴らしました。山猫がひげをぴんとひねって言いました。
「裁判ももうきょうで三日目だぞ。いい加減になかなおりをしたらどうだ。」
「いえ、いえ、だめです。あたまのとがったものが……。」がやがやがやがや。
　山ねこが叫びました。
「やかましい。ここをなんとこころえる。しずまれ、しずまれ。」別当が、むちをひゅうぱちっと鳴らし、どんぐりはみんなしずまりました。山猫が一郎にそっと申しました。
「このとおりです。どうしたらいいでしょう。」
　一郎はわらってこたえました。
「そんなら、こう言いわたしたらいいでしょう。このなかでいちばんばかで、めちゃくちゃで、まるでなっていないようなのが、いちばんえらいとね。ぼくお説教できいたんです。」
　山猫はなるほどというふうにうなずいて、それからいかにも気取って、繻子のきものの襟を開いて、黄いろの陣羽織をちょっと出してどんぐりどもに申しわたしました。
「よろしい。しずかにしろ。申しわたしだ。このなかで、いちばんえらくなくて、ばかで、めちゃくちゃで、てんでなっていなくて、あたまのつぶれたようなやつが、いちばんえらいのだ。」

"No, no, it's no good. Whatever you say, the one with the most pointed head's best!"

"No, you're wrong. The roundest one's best!"

"No, he's not, it's the biggest!"

Chatter, chatter, chatter again, till you had no idea what was going on.

"That's enough! Where do you think you are?" Wildcat shouted. "Silence! Silence!"

Swish, crack! went the coachman's whip again. Wildcat twisted his whiskers till they stood straight up, then started again.

"I don't need to remind you, this is the third day this case has been going on. Why don't you call it off and be friends again?"

"No, no, it's no good! The one with the most pointed head ..." Chatter, chatter, chatter....

"That's enough!" Wildcat yelled. "Where do you think you are? Silence! Silence!"

Again the coachman's whip went *swish, crack!* and again the acorns fell silent.

"You see what it's like," whispered Wildcat to Ichiro. "What do you think I ought to do?"

Ichiro smiled. "Well, here's one suggestion," he said. "Tell them that the best is the one who's most stupid, most ridiculous, and most good-for-nothing. I heard that in a sermon, actually."

Wildcat nodded wisely and prepared to give his verdict. Pulling open his satin gown at the neck so that the yellow brocade coat showed a little, he put on his grandest air. Then he spoke.

"Right! Be quiet now! Here is my verdict. The best of you is the one who is least important, most foolish,

どんぐりは、しいんとしてしまいました。それはそれはしいんとして、堅まってしまいました。

　そこで山猫は、黒い繻子の服を脱いで、額の汗を拭ぐいながら、一郎の手をとりました。別当も大よろこびで、五六ぺん、鞭をひゅうぱちっ、ひゅうぱちっ、ひゅうひゅうぱちっと鳴らしました。やまねこが言いました。

「どうもありがとうございました。これほどのひどい裁判を、まるで一分半でかたづけてくださいました。どうかこれからわたしの裁判所の、名誉判事になってください。これからも、葉書が行ったら、どうか来てくださいませんか。そのたびにお礼はいたします。」

「承知しました。お礼なんかいりませんよ。」

「いいえ、お礼はどうかとってください。わたしのじんかくにかかわりますから。そしてこれからは、葉書にかねた一郎どのと書いて、こちらを裁判所としますが、ようございますか。」

　一郎が「ええ、かまいません。」と申しますと、山猫はまだなにか言いたそうに、しばらくひげをひねって、眼をぱちぱちさせていましたが、とうとう決心したらしく言い出しました。

「それから、はがきの文句ですが、これからは、用事これありに付き、明日出頭すべしと書いてどうでしょう。」

　一郎はわらって言いました。

「さあ、なんだか変ですね。そいつだけはやめた方がいいでしょう。」

　山猫は、どうも言いようがまずかった、いかにも残念だというふうに、しばらくひげをひねったまま、下を向いていましたが、やっとあきらめて言いました。

「それでは、文句はいままでのとおりにしましょう。そこで今日のお礼ですが、あなたは黄金のどんぐり一升と、

most ridiculous, absolutely good-for-nothing, and completely crackbrained!"

A hush fell over the acorns, such a complete hush that you could have heard a pin drop.

Wildcat took off his black gown and, wiping the sweat from his forehead, shook Ichiro's hand, while the coachman cracked his whip five or six times for sheer joy.

"I'm most obliged to you," said Wildcat to Ichiro. "I must say, you've taken a most awkward case off my hands in not so much as a minute and a half. I do hope you'll act as an honorary judge in my court again in the future. If ever I send you a postcard from now on, please come, won't you? I'll see you're suitably rewarded every time."

"Of course I'll come," said Ichiro. "But I don't want any reward."

"Oh, no," objected Wildcat. "You must accept one. It's a matter of honor for me, you see. And from now on, I'll address the postcard to 'Ichiro Kaneta, Esq.,' and call this 'The Court'—is that all right?"

"That's fine," said Ichiro.

Wildcat was silent for a moment, twirling his whiskers as though there was something more he wanted to say. Then he seemed to take courage and went on:

"About the wording of the card—how would it be if I put it like this: 'Pertaining to certain business in hand, your presence in court is formally requested'?"

Ichiro smiled. "It sounds rather funny to me, somehow. Perhaps you'd better leave that bit out."

Wildcat gazed crestfallen at the ground, still twiddling his whiskers as though regretting that he hadn't

塩鮭のあたまと、どっちがおすきですか。」

「黄金のどんぐりがすきです。」

　山猫は、鮭の頭でなくて、まあよかったというように、口早に馬車別当に言いました。

「どんぐりを一升早くもってこい。一升にたりなかったら、めっきのどんぐりもまぜてこい。はやく。」

　別当は、さっきのどんぐりをますに入れて、はかって叫びました。

「ちょうど一升あります。」

　山ねこの陣羽織が風にばたばた鳴りました。そこで山ねこは、大きく延びあがって、めをつぶって、半分あくびをしながら言いました。

「よし、はやく馬車のしたくをしろ。」白い大きなきのこでこしらえた馬車が、ひっぱりだされました。そしてなんだかねずみいろの、おかしな形の馬がついています。

「さあ、おうちへお送りいたしましょう。」山猫が言いました。二人は馬車にのり別当は、どんぐりのますを馬車のなかに入れました。

　ひゅう、ぱちっ。

　馬車は草地をはなれました。木や藪がけむりのようにぐらぐらゆれました。一郎は黄金のどんぐりを見、山猫はとぼけたかおつきで、遠くをみていました。

　馬車が進むにしたがって、どんぐりはだんだん光がうすくなって、まもなく馬車がとまったときは、あたりまえの茶いろのどんぐりに変わっていました。そして、山猫の黄いろな陣羽織も、別当も、きのこの馬車も、一度に見えなくなって、一郎はじぶんのうちの前に、どんぐりを入れたますを持って立っていました。

　それからあと、山ねこ拝というはがきは、もうきませ

put it better. Finally, with a sigh, he said:

"Well, then, we'll leave it as it stands. Oh yes—about your reward for today. Which would you prefer, a pint of gold acorns or a salted salmon head?"

"The acorns, please," replied Ichiro.

Wildcat turned straight to his coachman, as if relieved that it hadn't been the salmon head.

"Get a pint of gold acorns," he said, speaking fast. "If there aren't enough, you can put in some gold-plated ones. And be quick about it!"

The coachman began to scoop the acorns into a square wooden measure. When he had finished, he shouted: "One pint exactly."

Wildcat's brocade coat flapped in the breeze. He stretched, closed his eyes, and smothered a yawn.

"Right!" he said. "Now hurry up and get the coach ready."

A carriage made of a great white mushroom appeared, drawn by a horse of a most peculiar shape and gray in color—just like a rat, in fact. Wildcat turned to Ichiro.

"And now we'll see you home," he said.

They got into the carriage, the coachman put the measure full of acorns in beside them, and—*swish, crack!*—off they went. The meadow was left behind, and trees and bushes swayed by in a bluish haze. Ichiro's eyes were fixed on his gold acorns, while Wildcat was gazing quite innocently into the distance.

But as the carriage journeyed on, the acorns lost their glitter, and when—in no time, it seemed—the carriage came to a halt, they were just the plain, ordinary, brown kind. Wildcat's yellow brocade coat, and the coachman, and the mushroom carriage—all had vanished together,

んでした。やっぱり、出頭すべしと書いてもいいと言え
ばよかったと、一郎はときどき思うのです。

and Ichiro was left standing in front of his own home, the measure of acorns in his hand.

From that time on, there were no more postcards signed "Yours respectfully, Wildcat." Ichiro sometimes wonders about it. Perhaps he ought to have let Wildcat write "your presence is formally requested," after all?

注文の多い料理店

　二人の若い紳士が、すっかりイギリスの兵隊のかたちをして、ぴかぴかする鉄砲をかついで、白熊のような犬を二疋つれて、だいぶ山奥の、木の葉のかさかさしたとこを、こんなことを言いながら、あるいておりました。

「ぜんたい、ここらの山は怪しからんね。鳥も獣も一疋も居やがらん。なんでも構わないから、早くタンタアーンと、やって見たいもんだなあ。」

「鹿の黄いろな横っ腹なんぞに、二三発お見舞いもうしたら、ずいぶん痛快だろうねえ。くるくるまわって、それからどたっと倒れるだろうねえ。」

　それはだいぶの山奥でした。案内してきた専門の鉄砲打ちも、ちょっとまごついて、どこかへ行ってしまったくらいの山奥でした。

　それに、あんまり山が物凄いので、その白熊のような犬が、二疋いっしょにめまいを起こして、しばらく吠って、それから泡を吐いて死んでしまいました。

「じつにぼくは、二千四百円の損害だ。」と一人の紳士が、その犬の眼ぶたを、ちょっとかえしてみて言いました。

「ぼくは二千八百円の損害だ。」と、もひとりが、くやしそうに、あたまをまげて言いました。

　はじめの紳士は、すこし顔いろを悪くして、じっと、もひとりの紳士の、顔つきを見ながら言いました。

The Restaurant of Many Orders

Two young gentlemen dressed just like British military men, with gleaming guns on their shoulders and two dogs like great white bears at their heels, were walking in the mountains where the leaves rustled dry underfoot. They were talking as they went.

"I must say, the country around here is really awful," said one. "Not a bird or beast in sight. I'm just dying to let fly at something: *bang, bang!* Anything, so long as it moves."

"Yes, what fun it would be to let a deer or something have a couple of shots smack in his tawny flank!" said the other. "I can just see him spinning around, then flopping down with a thud."

They really were *very* deep in the mountains. So deep, in fact, that the professional hunter who had come as their guide went astray and wandered off somewhere. Worse still, the forest was so frightening that the two bearlike dogs both got dizzy, howled for a while, then foamed at the mouth and died.

"Do you realize that dog cost me two thousand four hundred silver pieces?" said one young gentleman, casually turning its eyelids back.

"Mine cost me two thousand eight hundred," said the other, his head tilted ruefully to one side.

The first young gentleman went pale.

「ぼくはもう戻ろうとおもう。」

「さあ、ぼくもちょうど寒くはなったし腹は空いてきたし戻ろうとおもう。」

「そいじゃ、これで切りあげよう。なあに戻りに、昨日の宿屋で、山鳥を拾円も買って帰ればいい。」

「兎もでていたねえ。そうすれば結局おんなじこった。では帰ろうじゃないか。」

　ところがどうも困ったことは、どっちへ行けば戻れるのか、いっこう見当がつかなくなっていました。

　風がどうと吹いてきて、草はざわざわ、木の葉はかさかさ、木はごとんごとんと鳴りました。

「どうも腹が空いた。さっきから横っ腹が痛くてたまらないんだ。」

「ぼくもそうだ。もうあんまりあるきたくないな。」

「あるきたくないよ。ああ困ったなあ、何かたべたいなあ。」

「喰べたいもんだなあ。」

　二人の紳士は、ざわざわ鳴るすすきの中で、こんなことを言いました。

　その時ふとうしろを見ますと、立派な一軒の西洋造りの家がありました。

　そして玄関には

RESTAURANT　西洋料理店
WILDCAT HOUSE　山猫軒

という札がでていました。

「君、ちょうどいい。ここはこれでなかなか開けてるんだ。入ろうじゃないか。」

「おや、こんなとこにおかしいね。しかしとにかく何か食事ができるんだろう。」

"I think I'll be getting back," he said, gazing into the other's face.

"As a matter of fact," said his friend, "I was just beginning to get a bit cold and hungry myself, so I think I'll join you."

"Then let's call it a day. What does it matter? On our way back we can drop in at yesterday's inn and buy a few game birds to take home with us."

"They had hares too, didn't they? So it'll come to the same thing in the end. Well, why don't we go home, then?"

But the annoying thing was that by now they no longer had the faintest idea of the way back.

A sudden gust of wind sprang up; the grass stirred, the leaves rustled, and the trees creaked and groaned.

"I really am hungry!" said one. "I've had an awful hollow feeling under my ribs for quite a while."

"So have I," said the other. "I don't feel like walking any farther."

"O for something to eat!" said the first.

The pampas grass was rustling all about them as they talked.

Just then, one of them happened to look around, and what should he see standing there but a fine brick building. Over the entrance was a notice that said, in large letters:

RESTAURANT WILDCAT HOUSE

"Look! This is perfect," said one. "The place is civilized after all. Why don't we go in?"

"Funny," said the other, "finding it in a place like this. But I expect we'll be able to get a meal, at any rate."

「もちろんできるさ。看板にそう書いてあるじゃないか。」

「はいろうじゃないか。ぼくはもう何か喰べたくて倒れそうなんだ。」

二人は玄関に立ちました。玄関は白い瀬戸の煉瓦で組んで、実に立派なもんです。

そして硝子の開き戸がたって、そこに金文字でこう書いてありました。

「どなたもどうかお入りください。決してご遠慮はありません。」

二人はそこで、ひどくよろこんで言いました。

「こいつはどうだ、やっぱり世の中はうまくできてるねえ、きょう一日なんぎしたけれど、こんどはこんないいこともある。このうちは料理店だけれどもただでご馳走するんだぜ。」

「どうもそうらしい。決してご遠慮ありませんというのはその意味だ。」

二人は戸を押して、なかへ入りました。そこはすぐ廊下になっていました。その硝子戸の裏側には、金文字でこうなっていました。

「ことに肥ったお方や若いお方は、大歓迎いたします。」

二人は大歓迎というので、もう大よろこびです。

「君、ぼくらは大歓迎にあたっているのだ。」

「ぼくらは両方兼ねてるから。」

ずんずん廊下を進んで行きますと、こんどは水いろのペンキ塗りの扉がありました。

"Of course we will, silly. What do you think the sign means?"

"Let's give it a try. I'm just about collapsing with hunger."

They stepped into the entrance hall, which was very splendid, being done all over in white tiles. There was a glass door, with something written on it in gold letters.

PLEASE COME IN. NO ONE NEED HAVE A MOMENT'S HESITATION.

They were tickled pink.

"Just look at that!" said one of them. "Things always turn out right in the end. Everything's been going wrong all day, but look how lucky we are now. They're telling us not to worry about the bill!"

"I must say, it does seem like it," said the other. "That's what 'no one need have a moment's hesitation' suggests."

They pushed open the door and went through. On the other side was a corridor. Another notice in gold letters on the back of the glass door said:

PLUMP PARTIES AND YOUNG PARTIES ESPECIALLY WELCOME.

They were both overjoyed at this.

"Look, we're especially welcome, it says," said one.

"Because we satisfy both conditions!" said the other.

They walked briskly along the corridor and came to another door, this time painted bright blue.

"What a strange place! I wonder why there are so many doors?"

"This is the Russian way of doing things, of course.

「どうも変な家だ。どうしてこんなにたくさん戸があるのだろう。」

「これはロシア式だ。寒いとこや山の中はみんなこうさ。」

　そして二人はその扉をあけようとしますと、上に黄いろな字でこう書いてありました。

「当軒は注文の多い料理店ですからどうかそこはご承知ください。」

「なかなかはやってるんだ。こんな山の中で。」

「それぁそうだ。見たまえ、東京の大きな料理屋だって大通りにはすくないだろう。」

　二人は言いながら、その扉をあけました。するとその裏側に、

「注文はずいぶん多いでしょうがどうか一々こらえて下さい。」

「これはぜんたいどういうんだ。」ひとりの紳士は顔をしかめました。

「うん、これはきっと注文があまり多くて支度が手間取るけれどもごめん下さいと斯ういうことだ。」

「そうだろう。早くどこか室の中にはいりたいもんだな。」

「そしてテーブルに座りたいもんだな。」

　ところがどうもうるさいことは、また扉が一つありました。そしてそのわきに鏡がかかって、その下には長い柄のついたブラシが置いてあったのです。

　扉には赤い字で、

It's always like this in cold places or in the mountains."

They were just going to open the door when they saw a notice in yellow letters above it:

WE HOPE YOU WILL APPRECIATE THAT THIS IS A RESTAURANT OF MANY ORDERS.

"Awfully popular, isn't it? Out here in the mountains like this!"

"But of course. Why, even back in the capital very few of the best restaurants are on the main streets, are they?"

As they were talking, they opened the door. A notice on the other side said:

THERE REALLY ARE RATHER A LOT OF ORDERS, BUT WE HOPE YOU WILL BE PATIENT.

"Now just what does that mean?" said one young gentleman, screwing up his face.

"Mm—I suppose it means they're busy, and they're sorry but it will be a while before the food appears. Something like that."

"I expect so. I want to get settled down in a room as soon as possible, don't you?"

"Yes, and ready to tuck in."

But it was most frustrating—there was yet another door, and by the side of it hung a mirror, with a long-handled brush lying beneath it. On the door it said in red letters:

PATRONS ARE REQUESTED TO COMB THEIR HAIR AND GET THE MUD OFF THEIR BOOTS HERE.

"Very right and proper, too. And back in the hall just now I was thinking this was just a place for the locals."

「お客さまがた、ここで髪をきちんとして、それからはきものの泥を落としてください。」

と書いてありました。
　「これはどうも尤もだ。僕もさっき玄関で、山のなかだとおもって見くびったんだよ。」
　「作法の厳しい家だ。きっとよほど偉い人たちが、たびたび来るんだ。」
　そこで二人は、きれいに髪をけずって、靴の泥を落としました。
　そしたら、どうです。ブラシを板の上に置くや否や、そいつがぼうっとかすんで無くなって、風がどうっと室の中に入ってきました。
　二人はびっくりして、互いによりそって、扉をがたんと開けて、次の室へ入って行きました。早く何か暖かいものでもたべて、元気をつけて置かないと、もう途方もないことになってしまうと、二人とも思ったのでした。
　扉の内側に、また変なことが書いてありました。

　「鉄砲と弾丸をここへ置いてください。」

　見るとすぐ横に黒い台がありました。
　「なるほど、鉄砲を持ってものを食うという法はない。」
　「いや、よほど偉いひとが始終来ているんだ。」
　二人は鉄砲をはずし、帯皮を解いて、それを台の上に置きました。
　また黒い扉がありました。

　「どうか帽子と外套と靴をおとり下さい。」

"They're very strict on etiquette. Some of their customers must be rather grand."

So they neatly combed their hair and got the mud off their boots.

But no sooner had they put the brush back on its shelf than it blurred and disappeared, and a sudden gust of wind moaned through the room. They huddled together in alarm and, flinging the door open, went into the next room. Both of them felt that unless they fortified themselves with something warm to eat very soon, almost anything might happen.

On the other side of the door there was another unexpected sign:

PLEASE LEAVE YOUR GUNS AND CARTRIDGES HERE.

Sure enough, there was a black gun rack right by the door.

"Of course," said one young gentleman. "No one ever ate with his gun."

"I'm beginning to think their customers must *all* be rather grand," said the other.

They unshouldered their guns and unbuckled their belts and put them on the rack. Now there was another door, a black one, which said:

KINDLY REMOVE YOUR HATS, OVERCOATS, AND BOOTS.

"What about it—do we take them off?"

"I suppose we'd better. They really must be *very* grand, the people dining there in the back rooms.

They hung their hats and overcoats on the hook, then took their boots off and padded on through the door. On the other side was the notice:

PLEASE REMOVE YOUR TIEPINS, CUFF LINKS, SPECTA-

「どうだ、とるか。」

「仕方ない、とろう。たしかによっぽどえらいひとなんだ。奥に来ているのは。」

　二人は帽子とオーバーコートを釘にかけ、靴をぬいでぺたぺたあるいて扉の中にはいりました。

　扉の裏側には、

「ネクタイピン、カフスボタン、眼鏡、財布、その他金物類、ことに尖ったものは、みんなここに置いてください。」

と書いてありました。扉のすぐ横には黒塗りの立派な金庫も、ちゃんと口を開けて置いてありました。鍵まで添えてあったのです。

「ははあ、何かの料理に電気をつかうと見えるね。金気のものはあぶない。ことに尖ったものはあぶないと斯う言うんだろう。」

「そうだろう。して見ると勘定は帰りにここで払うのだろうか。」

「どうもそうらしい。」

「そうだ。きっと。」

二人はめがねをはずしたり、カフスボタンをとったり、みんな金庫の中に入れて、ぱちんと錠をかけました。

　すこし行きますとまた扉があって、その前に硝子の壺が一つありました。扉には斯う書いてありました。

「壺のなかのクリームを顔や手足にすっかり塗ってください。」

　みるとたしかに壺のなかのものは牛乳のクリームでした。

「クリームをぬれというのはどういうんだ。」

CLES, PURSES, AND ANYTHING ELSE WITH METAL IN IT, ESPECIALLY ANYTHING POINTED.

Right by the door a fine black safe stood open and waiting. It even had a lock on it.

"Of course! I imagine they use electricity at some point in the cooking. So metal things are dangerous, especially pointed things. I expect that's what it means."

"I suppose so. I wonder if it also means you pay the bill here on the way out?"

"It seems like it, doesn't it?"

"Yes, that must be it."

They took off their spectacles and their cuff links and so on, put everything in the safe, and clicked the lock shut.

A little farther on, they came to another door, with a glass jar standing in front of it. On the door it said:

PLEASE SPREAD CREAM FROM THE JAR ALL OVER YOUR FACE, HANDS, AND FEET.

"Why should they want one to put cream on?"

"Well, if it's very cold outside and too warm inside, one's skin gets chapped, so this is to prevent it. I must say, it does seem they only get the very best sort of people coming here. At this rate, we may soon be on speaking terms with the aristocracy!"

They rubbed some cream from the jar on their faces and hands, then took their socks off and rubbed it on their feet as well. Even so, there was still a bit left, so they both ate some surreptitiously, pretending to be rubbing it on their faces all the while.

Then they opened the door in a great hurry—only to find a notice on the other side which said:

「これはね、外がひじょうに寒いだろう。室のなかがあんまり暖かいとひびがきれるから、その予防なんだ。どうも奥には、よほどえらいひとがきている。こんなとこで、案外ぼくらは、貴族とちかづきになるかも知れないよ。」

　二人は壺のクリームを、顔に塗って手に塗ってそれから靴下をぬいで足に塗りました。それでもまだ残っていましたから、それは二人ともめいめいこっそり顔へ塗るふりをしながら喰べました。

　それから大急ぎで扉をあけますと、その裏側には、

「クリームをよく塗りましたか、耳にもよく塗りましたか。」

と書いてあって、ちいさなクリームの壺がここにも置いてありました。

「そうそう、ぼくは耳には塗らなかった。あぶなく耳にひびを切らすとこだった。ここの主人はじつに用意周到だね。」

「ああ、細かいとこまでよく気がつくよ。ところでぼくは早く何か喰べたいんだが、どうも斯うどこまでも廊下じゃ仕方ないね。」

　するとすぐその前に次の戸がありました。

　　「料理はもうすぐできます。
　　十五分とお待たせはいたしません。
　　すぐたべられます。
　　早くあなたの頭に瓶の中の香水をよく振りかけてください。」

There was another, smaller jar of cream here.

"Of course—I didn't do my ears. I might well have got them chapped. The proprietor of this place is really very thoughtful."

"Yes, he's got an eye for every little detail. Incidentally, I wouldn't mind something to eat, but it doesn't look very likely with all these eternal corridors, does it?"

But the next door was already upon them, bearing another message:

THE MEAL WILL SOON BE READY. WE WON'T KEEP YOU AS MUCH AS FIFTEEN MINUTES. IN THE MEANTIME, JUST SHAKE SOME OF THIS PERFUME OVER YOUR HEAD.

And there in front of the door stood a shiny gold bottle of scent.

Unfortunately, when they splashed some on themselves, it smelled suspiciously like vinegar.

"This stuff's awfully vinegary," said one young gentleman. "What's wrong with it, do you suppose?"

"They've made a mistake," the other said. "The maid must have had a cold or something and put the wrong stuff in."

They opened the door and went through. On the other side of it was a notice in big letters that said:

YOU MUST BE TIRED OF ALL THESE ORDERS, YOU POOR THINGS. THIS IS THE LAST ONE, SO BE GOOD ENOUGH TO TAKE SOME SALT FROM THE POT AND RUB IT IN WELL ALL OVER YOU.

そして戸の前には金ピカの香水の瓶が置いてありました。

二人はその香水を、頭へぱちゃぱちゃ振りかけました。

ところがその香水は、どうも酢のような匂いがするのでした。

「この香水はへんに酢くさい。どうしたんだろう。」

「まちがえたんだ。下女が風邪でも引いてまちがえて入れたんだ。」

二人は扉をあけて中にはいりました。

扉の裏側には、大きな字で斯う書いてありました。

「いろいろ注文が多くてうるさかったでしょう。お気の毒でした。もうこれだけです。どうかからだ中に、壺の中の塩をたくさんよくもみ込んでください。」

なるほど立派な青い瀬戸の塩壺は置いてありましたが、こんどというこんどは二人ともぎょっとしてお互いにクリームをたくさん塗った顔を見合わせました。

「どうもおかしいぜ。」

「ぼくもおかしいとおもう。」

「沢山の注文というのは、向こうがこっちへ注文してるんだよ。」

「だからさ、西洋料理店というのは、ぼくの考えるところでは、西洋料理を、来た人にたべさせるのではなくて、来た人を西洋料理にして、食べてやる家とこういうことなんだ。これは、その、つ、つ、つ、つまり、ぼ、ぼ、ぼくらが……。」がたがたがたがた、ふるえだしてもうものが言えませんでした。

「その、ぼ、ぼくらが、……うわあ。」がたがたがたがたふるえだして、もうものが言えませんでした。

58

A fine blue china salt cellar was indeed standing there, but this time both the young gentlemen were thoroughly alarmed. They turned their cream-smeared faces to look at one another.

"I don't like the look of this," said one.

"Nor do I," said the other.

"'Lots of orders' means *they're* giving *us* orders."

"Yes—and I've an idea that 'restaurant' doesn't mean a place for serving food, but a place for cooking people and serving *them*. And that m-m-means that w-w-we ..."

He began to shake and tremble, and tremble and shake, so that he couldn't go on.

"Then w-w-we ... Oh *dear* ! " And the other one, too, began to quake and shiver, and shiver and quake, so that he couldn't go on either.

"Let's get out!" Still shaking all over, one of the young gentlemen pushed at the door behind him. But, strange to say, it refused to budge.

At the other end was another door with two big keyholes and a silver knife and fork carved on it. It said:

So NICE OF YOU TO COME. THAT WILL DO VERY NICELY INDEED. NOW JUST POP INSIDE, PLEASE.

What was worse, two blue eyeballs were ogling them through the keyhole.

"Oh dear!" cried one, quivering and trembling.

"Oh *dear*!" cried the other, trembling and quivering.

And they both burst into tears.

Just then, they heard voices talking furtively on the other side of the door.

「逃げ……。」がたがたしながら一人の紳士はうしろの戸を押そうとしましたが、どうです、戸はもう一分も動きませんでした。

　奥の方にはまだ一枚扉があって、大きなかぎ穴が二つつき、銀いろのホークとナイフの形が切りだしてあって、

「いや、わざわざご苦労です。

　　大へん結構にできました。

　　さあさあおなかにおはいりください。」

と書いてありました。おまけにかぎ穴からはきょろきょろ二つの青い眼玉がこっちをのぞいています。

「うわあ。」がたがたがたがた。

「うわあ。」がたがたがたがた。

　ふたりは泣き出しました。

　すると戸の中では、こそこそこんなことを言っています。

「だめだよ。もう気がついたよ。塩をもみこまないようだよ。」

「あたりまえさ。親分の書きようがまずいんだ。あすこへ、いろいろ注文が多くてうるさかったでしょう、お気の毒でしたなんて、間抜けなことを書いたもんだ。」

「どっちでもいいよ。どうせぼくらには、骨も分けて呉れやしないんだ。」

「それはそうだ。けれどももしここへあいつらがはいって来なかったら、それはぼくらの責任だぜ。」

「呼ぼうか、呼ぼう。おい、お客さん方、早くいらっしゃい。いらっしゃい。いらっしゃい。お皿も洗ってありますし、菜っ葉ももうよく塩でもんで置きました。あとはあなたがたと、菜っ葉をうまくとりあわせて、まっ白

"It's no good—they've realized. It doesn't look as if they're going to rub in the salt."

"What d'you expect? The way the boss put it was all wrong—'you poor things' and the like—stupid, I call it."

"Who cares? Either way, *we* won't get as much as the bones even."

"How right you are. But if they won't come in here, it's us who'll get the blame."

"Shall we call them? Yes, let's. Hey, gentlemen! This way, quickly—this way! The dishes are washed, and the vegetables nicely salted. All that's left is to arrange you nicely with the greens and put you on some snowy white dishes. This way now, quickly!"

The two young gentlemen were so distressed that their faces went all crumpled like pieces of wastepaper.

なお皿にのせるだけです。はやくいらっしゃい。」

「へい、いらっしゃい、いらっしゃい。それともサラドはお嫌いですか。そんならこれから火を起こしてフライにしてあげましょうか。とにかくはやくいらっしゃい。」

二人はあんまり心を痛めたために、顔がまるでくしゃくしゃの紙屑のようになり、お互いにその顔を見合わせ、ぶるぶるふるえ、声もなく泣きました。

中ではふっふっとわらってまた叫んでいます。
「いらっしゃい、いらっしゃい。そんなに泣いては折角のクリームが流れるじゃありませんか。へい、ただいま。じきもってまいります。さあ、早くいらっしゃい。」
「早くいらっしゃい。親方がもうナフキンをかけて、ナイフをもって、舌なめずりして、お客さま方を待っていられます。」

二人は泣いて泣いて泣いて泣いて泣きました。

そのときうしろからいきなり、
「わん、わん、ぐゎあ。」という声がして、あの白熊のような犬が二疋、扉をつきやぶって室の中に飛び込んできました。鍵穴の眼玉はたちまちなくなり、犬どもはうううとうなってしばらく室の中をくるくる廻っていましたが、また一声、
「わん。」と高く吠えて、いきなり次の扉に飛びつきました。戸はがたりとひらき、犬どもは吸い込まれるように飛んで行きました。

その扉の向こうのまっくらやみのなかで、
「にゃあお。くゎあ、ごろごろ。」という声がして、それからがさがさ鳴りました。

室はけむりのように消え、二人は寒さにぶるぶるふるえて、草の中に立っていました。

They peered at each other and shook and shivered and silently wept.

There were chuckles on the other side of the door, then a voice shouted again, "This way, this way! If you cry like that, you know, you'll wash off all the cream you put on specially. (Yes, sir, coming, sir. We'll be bringing it in just a moment, sir.) Come on, we haven't got all day!"

"Yes, hurry up! The boss has his napkin tucked in and his knife in his hand and he's licking his lips, just waiting for you."

But the two young gentlemen just wept and wept and wept and wept.

Then, all of a sudden, they heard a *woof, woof*, and a *grr!* behind them, and the two dogs like white bears came bursting into the room. The eyes behind the keyholes disappeared in a twinkling. Round and round the room the dogs rushed, snarling, then with another great *woof!* they threw themselves at the other door. The door banged open, and they vanished inside as though swallowed up. From the pitch darkness beyond came a great miaowing and spitting and growling, then a rustling sound.

The room vanished in a puff of smoke, and the two young gentlemen found themselves standing in the grass, shivering and shaking in the cold. Their coats and boots, purses and tiepins were all there with them, hanging from the branches or lying among the roots of the trees. A gust of wind set the grass stirring, the leaves rustling, and the trees creaking and groaning.

The dogs came back, panting, and behind them someone called, "Gentlemen! Gentlemen!"

"Hey! Hey!" they shouted, suddenly recovering their spirits. "We're over here. This way, quickly!"

見ると、上着や靴や財布やネクタイピンは、あっちの枝にぶらさがったり、こっちの根もとにちらばったりしています。風がどうと吹いてきて、草はざわざわ、木の葉はかさかさ、木はごとんごとんと鳴りました。

　犬がふうとうなって戻ってきました。

　そしてうしろからは、

「旦那あ、旦那あ、」と叫ぶものがあります。

　二人は俄かに元気がついて、

「おおい、おおい、ここだぞ、早く来い。」と叫びました。

　蓑帽子をかぶった専門の猟師が、草をざわざわ分けてやってきました。

　そこで二人はやっと安心しました。

　そして猟師のもってきた団子をたべ、途中で十円だけ山鳥を買って東京に帰りました。

　しかし、さっき一ぺん紙くずのようになった二人の顔だけは、東京に帰っても、お湯にはいっても、もうもとのとおりになおりませんでした。

The professional hunter in his straw cape came rustling toward them through the grass, and they really felt safe at last.

They ate the dumplings the guide had brought with him, then returned to the capital, buying some game birds on their way.

But even back in the capital, and however long they soaked themselves in hot baths, their faces that had gone all crumpled like wastepaper would never go back to normal again.

土神ときつね

（一）

　一本木の野原の、北のはずれに、少し小高く盛りあがった所がありました。いのころぐさがいっぱいに生え、そのまん中には一本の奇麗な女の樺の木がありました。

　それはそんなに大きくはありませんでしたが幹はてかてか黒く光り、枝は美しく伸びて、五月には白い花を雲のようにつけ、秋は黄金や紅やいろいろの葉を降らせました。

　ですから渡り鳥のかっこうや百舌も、また小さなみそさざいや目白もみんなこの木に停まりました。ただもしも若い鷹などが来ているときは小さな鳥は遠くからそれを見付けて決して近くへ寄りませんでした。

　この木に二人の友達がありました。一人は丁度、五百歩ばかり離れたぐちゃぐちゃの谷地の中に住んでいる土神で一人はいつも野原の南の方からやって来る茶いろの狐だったのです。

　樺の木はどちらかと言えば狐の方がすきでした。なぜなら土神の方は神という名こそついてはいましたがごく乱暴で髪もぼろぼろの木綿糸の束のよう眼も赤くきものだってまるでわかめに似、いつもはだしで爪も黒く長いのでした。ところが狐の方は大へんに上品な風で滅多に人を怒らせたり気にさわるようなことをしなかったのです。

The Earthgod and the Fox

*

On the northern edge of a stretch of open land the ground rose in a slight hillock. The hillock was covered entirely with spike-eared grass, and right in the middle of it stood a single, beautiful female birch tree.

The tree was not actually very big, but her trunk gleamed a glossy black and her branches spread out gracefully. In May her pale flowers were like clouds, while in autumn she shed leaves of gold and crimson and many other colors.

All the birds, from birds of passage such as the cuckoo and the shrike right down to the tiny wren and the white-eye, would come to perch in the tree. But if a young hawk or some other large bird was there, the smaller birds would spy him from afar and refuse to go anywhere near.

The tree had two friends. One was the earthgod, who lived in the middle of a marshy hollow about five hundred paces away, and the other was a brown fox, who always appeared from somewhere in the southern part of the plain.

Of the two of them it was the fox, perhaps, that the birch tree preferred. The earthgod, in spite of his imposing name, was too wild, with hair hanging unkempt like a bundle of ragged cotton thread, bloodshot eyes, and clothes that dangled about him like bits of seaweed. He always went barefoot, and his nails were long and black.

ただもしよくよくこの二人をくらべて見たら土神の方は正直で狐は少し不正直だったかも知れません。

(二)

　夏のはじめのある晩でした。樺には新しい柔らかな葉がいっぱいについていいかおりがそこら中いっぱい、空にはもう天の川がしらしらと渡り星はいちめんふるえたりゆれたり灯ったり消えたりしていました。
　その下を狐が詩集をもって遊びに行ったのでした。仕立ておろしの紺の背広を着、赤革の靴もキッキッと鳴ったのです。
「実にしずかな晩ですねえ。」
「ええ。」樺の木はそっと返事をしました。
「蝎ぼしが向こうを這っていますね。あの赤い大きなやつを昔は支那では火と言ったんですよ。」
「火星とはちがうんでしょうか。」
「火星とはちがいますよ。火星は惑星ですね、ところがあいつは立派な恒星なんです。」
「惑星、恒星ってどういうんですの。」
「惑星というのはですね、自分で光らないやつです。つまりほかから光を受けてやっと光るように見えるんです。恒星の方は自分で光るやつなんです。お日さまなんかは勿論恒星ですね。あんなに大きくてまぶしいんですがもし途方もない遠くから見たらやっぱり小さな星に見えるんでしょうね。」
「まあ、お日さまも星のうちだったんですわね。そうして見ると空にはずいぶん沢山のお日さまが、あら、お星さまが、あらやっぱり変だわ、お日さまがあるんですね。」
　狐は鷹揚に笑いました。
「まあそうです。」

The fox, on the other hand, was very refined and almost never made people angry or offended.

The only thing was that, if you compared them really carefully, the earthgod was honest, whereas the fox was, perhaps, just a bit dishonest.

*

It was an evening at the beginning of summer. The birch tree was covered with soft new leaves, which filled the air around them with a delightful fragrance. The Milky Way stretched whitish across the sky, and the stars were winking and blinking and switching themselves on and off all over the firmament.

On such a night, then, the fox came to pay the birch tree a visit, bringing with him a book of poetry. He was wearing a dark blue suit fresh from the tailor's, and his light brown leather shoes squeaked slightly as he walked.

"What a peaceful night," he said.

"Oh, yes!" breathed the birch tree.

"Do you see Scorpio crawling across the sky over there? In ancient China, you know, they used to call the big red star in the constellation the 'Fire Star.'"

"Would that be the same as Mars?"

"Dear me, no. Not Mars. Mars is a *planet*. This one is a real star."

"Then what's the difference between a planet and a star?"

"Why, a planet can't shine by itself. In other words, it has to have light from somewhere else before it can be seen. A star is the kind that shines by itself. The sun, now, is a star, of course. It looks big and dazzling to us, but if you saw it from very far away, it would only look like a small star, just the same as all the others."

「お星さまにはどうしてああ赤いのや黄のや緑のやあるんでしょうね。」

　狐はまた鷹揚に笑って腕を高く組みました。詩集はぷらぷらしましたがなかなかそれで落ちませんでした。

「星に橙や青やいろいろある訳ですが、それは斯うです。全体星というものははじめはぼんやりした雲のようなものだったんです。いまの空にも沢山あります。たとえばアンドロメダにもオリオンにも猟犬座にもみんなあります。猟犬座のは渦巻きです。それから環状星雲というのもあります。魚の口の形ですから魚口星雲とも言いますね。そんなのが今の空にも沢山あるんです。」

「まあ、あたしいつか見たいわ。魚の口の形の星だなんてまあどんなに立派でしょう。」

「それは立派ですよ。僕水沢の天文台で見ましたがね。」

「まあ、あたしも見たいわ。」

「見せてあげましょう。僕実は望遠鏡を独乙のツァイスに注文してあるんです。来年の春までには来ますから来たらすぐ見せてあげましょう。」狐は思わず斯う言ってしまいました。そしてすぐ考えたのです。ああ僕はたった一人のお友達にまたつい偽を言ってしまった。ああ僕はほんとうにだめなやつだ。けれども決して悪い気で言ったんじゃない。よろこばせようと思って言ったんだ。あとですっかり本当のことを言ってしまおう、狐はしばらくしんとしながら斯う考えていたのでした。樺の木はそんなことも知らないでよろこんで言いました。

「まあうれしい。あなた本当にいつでも親切だわ。」

　狐は少し悄気ながら答えました。

「ええ、そして僕はあなたの為ならばほかのどんなことでもやりますよ。この詩集、ごらんなさいませんか。

"Good heavens! So the sun is only one of the stars, is it? Then I suppose the sky must have an awful lot of suns—no, stars—oh, silly me, *suns*, of course."

The fox smiled magnanimously. "You might put it like that," he said.

"I wonder why some stars are red, and some yellow, and some green?"

The fox smiled magnanimously again and folded his arms grandly across his chest. The book of poetry under his arm dangled perilously, but somehow stopped just short of falling.

"Well, you see," he said, "at first all the stars were like big, fluffy clouds. There are still lots of them like that in the sky. There are some in Andromeda, some in Orion, and some in the Hunting Dogs. Some of them are spiral-shaped and some are in rings the shape of fishes' mouths."

"I'd love to see them sometime. Stars the shape of fishes' mouths—how splendid!"

"Oh, they are, I can tell you. I saw them at the observatory."

"My word! I'd love to see them myself."

"I'll show you them. As a matter of fact, I've a telescope on order from Germany. It'll be here sometime before next spring, so I'll let you have a look as soon as it comes."

The fox had spoken without thinking, but the very next moment he was saying to himself, "Oh dear, if I haven't gone and told my only friend another fib again. But I only said it to please her, I really didn't mean any harm by it. Later on, I'll tell her the truth."

The fox was quiet for a while, occupied with such thoughts, but the birch tree was too delighted to notice.

ハイネという人のですよ。翻訳ですけれども仲々よくできてるんです。」

「まあ、お借りしていいんでしょうかしら。」

「構いませんとも。どうかゆっくりごらんなすって。じゃ僕もう失礼します。はてな、何か言い残したことがあるようだ。」

「お星さまのいろのことですわ。」

「ああそうそう、だけどそれは今度にしましょう。僕あんまり永くお邪魔しちゃいけないから。」

「あら、いいんですよ。」

「僕又来ますから、じゃさよなら。本はあげてきます。じゃ、さよなら。」狐はいそがしく帰って行きました。そして樺の木はその時吹いて来た南風にざわざわ葉を鳴らしながら狐の置いて行った詩集をとりあげて天の川やそらいちめんの星から来る微かなあかりにすかして頁を繰りました。そのハイネの詩集にはロウレライやさまざま美しい歌がいっぱいにあったのです。そして樺の木は一晩中よみ続けました。ただその野原の三時すぎ東から金牛宮ののぼるころ少しとろとろしただけでした。

　夜があけました。太陽がのぼりました。

　草には露がきらめき花はみな力いっぱい咲きました。

　その東北の方から熔けた銅の汁をからだ中に被ったように朝日をいっぱいに浴びて土神がゆっくりゆっくりやって来ました。いかにも分別くさそうに腕を拱きながらゆっくりゆっくりやって来たのでした。

　樺の木はなんだか少し困ったように思いながらそれでも青い葉をきらきらと動かして土神の来る方を向きました。その影は草に落ちてちらちらちらちらゆれました。

"I'm so happy!" she said. "You're always so kind to me."

"Oh, quite," said the fox rather dejectedly. "You know I'd do anything for you. Would you care to read this book of poetry, by the way? It's by a man called Heine. It's only a translation, of course, but it's not at all bad."

"Oh! May I really borrow it?"

"By all means. Take as long as you like over it.... Well, I must say goodbye now. Dear me, though, I feel there's something I forgot to say.

"Yes, about the color of the stars."

"Ah, of course! But let's leave that until next time, shall we? I mustn't overstay my welcome."

"Oh, that doesn't matter."

"Anyway, I'll be coming again soon. Goodbye to you, then. I'll leave the book with you. Goodbye."

The fox set off briskly homeward. And the birch tree, her leaves rustling in a south wind that sprang up just then, took up the book of verse and turned the pages in the light of the faint glow from the Milky Way and the stars that dotted the sky. The book contained "Lorelei" and many other beautiful poems by Heine, and the birch tree read on and on through the night. Not until past three, when Taurus was already beginning to climb in the east above the plain, did she begin to get even slightly drowsy.

Dawn broke, and the sun rose in the heavens. The dew glittered on the grass, and the flowers bloomed with all their might. Slowly, slowly, from the northeast, bathed in morning sunlight as though he had poured molten copper all over himself, came the earthgod. He walked slowly, quite slowly, with his arms folded soberly across his chest.

土神はしずかにやって来て樺の木の前に立ちました。
「樺の木さん。お早う。」
「お早うございます。」
「わしはね、どうも考えて見るとわからんことが沢山ある、なかなかわからんことが多いもんだね。」
「まあ、どんなことでございますの。」
「たとえばだね、草というものは黒い土から出るのだがなぜこう青いもんだろう。黄や白の花さえ咲くんだ。どうもわからんねえ。」
「それは草の種子が青や白をもっているためではないでございましょうか。」
「そうだ。まあそう言えばそうだがそれでもやっぱりわからんな。たとえば秋のきのこのようなものは種子もなし全く土の中からばかり出て行くもんだ。それにもやっぱり赤や黄いろやいろいろある、わからんねえ。」
「狐さんにでも聞いて見ましたらいかがでございましょう。」
　樺の木はうっとり昨夜の星のはなしをおもっていましたのでつい斯う言ってしまいました。
　この語を聞いて土神は俄かに顔いろを変えました。そしてこぶしを握りました。
「何だ。狐？　狐が何を言い居った。」
　樺の木はおろおろ声になりました。
「何も仰っしゃったんではございませんがちょっとしたらご存知かと思いましたので。」
「狐なんぞに神が物を教わるとは一体何たることだ。えい。」
　樺の木はもうすっかり恐くなってぷりぷりぷりぷりゆれました。土神は歯をきしきし嚙みながら高く腕を組んでそこらをあるきまわりました。その影はまっ黒に草に

Somehow, the birch tree felt rather put out, but even so she shimmered her bright green leaves in the earth-god's direction as he came, so that her shadow went flutter, flutter where it fell on the grass. The earthgod came up quietly and stopped in front of her.

"Good morning to you, Birch Tree."

"Good morning."

"D'you know, Birch Tree, there are lots of things I don't understand when I come to think about them. We don't really know very much, do we?"

"What kind of things?"

"Well, there's grass, for instance. Why should it be green, when it comes out of dark brown soil? And then there are the yellow and white flowers. It's all beyond me."

"Mightn't it be that the seeds of the grass have green or white inside them already?" said the birch tree.

"Yes. Yes, I suppose that's possible," he said. "But even so, it's beyond me. Take the toadstools in autumn, now. They come straight out of the earth without any seeds or anything. And they come up in red and yellow and all kinds of colors. I just don't understand it!"

"How would it be if you asked Mr. Fox?" said the birch tree, who was still too excited about last night's talk to know any better.

The earthgod's face changed color abruptly, and he clenched his fists.

"What's that? Fox? What's the fox been saying?"

"Oh," said the birch tree in a faltering voice, "he didn't say anything, really. It was just that I thought he might know."

"And what makes you think a fox has got anything to teach a god, eh?"

落ち草も恐れて顫えたのです。
「狐の如きは実に世の害悪だ。ただ一言もまことはなく卑怯で臆病でそれに非常に妬み深いのだ。うぬ、畜生の分際として。」

　樺の木はやっと気をとり直して言いました。
「もうあなたの方のお祭りも近づきましたね。」
　土神は少し顔色を和らげました。
「そうじゃ。今日は五月三日、あと六日だ。」
　土神はしばらく考えていましたが俄かに又声を暴らげました。
「しかしながら人間どもは不届きだ。近頃はわしの祭りにも供物一つ持って来ん、おのれ、今度わしの領分に最初に足を入れたものはきっと泥の底に引き擦り込んでやろう。」土神はまたきりきり歯嚙みしました。

　樺の木は折角なだめようと思って言ったことが又もや却ってこんなことになったのでもうどうしたらいいかわからなくなりただちらちらとその葉を風にゆすっていました。土神は日光を受けてまるで燃えるようになりながら高く腕を組みキリキリ歯嚙みをしてその辺をうろうろしていましたが考えれば考えるほど何もかもしゃくにさわって来るらしいのでした。そしてとうとうこらえ切れなくなって、吠えるようにうなって荒々しく自分の谷地に帰って行ったのでした。

(三)

　土神の棲んでいる所は小さな競馬場ぐらいある、冷たい湿地で苔やからくさやみじかい蘆などが生えていましたが又所々にはあざみやせいの低いひどくねじれた楊などもありました。

By now the birch tree was so unnerved that she could only quiver and quiver. The earthgod paced about with his arms folded over his chest, grinding his teeth loudly all the while. Even the grass shivered with fear wherever his jet-black shadow fell on it.

"That fox is a blight on the face of the earth!" he said. "Not a word of truth in him. Servile, cowardly, and terribly envious into the bargain! And him just animal!"

"It will soon be time for the yearly festival at your shrine, won't it?" said the birch tree, regaining her composure at last.

The earthgod's expression softened slightly.

"That's right," he said. "Today's the third of the month, so there are only six days to go."

But then he thought for a while and suddenly burst out again.

"Human beings, though, are a useless lot! They don't bring a single offering for my festival nowadays. Why, the next one that sets foot on my territory, I'll drag down to the bottom of the swamp for his pains!"

He stood there gnashing his teeth noisily. The birch tree, alarmed at finding that her attempts to soothe him had had just the opposite effect again, was past doing anything except fluttering her leaves in the breeze. For a while the earthgod strode about grinding his teeth, his arms folded high across his chest and his whole body seeming to blaze as the sunlight poured down on him. But the more he thought about it, the crosser he seemed to get. In the end he could bear it no longer and with a great howl stormed off home to his hollow.

*

The place where the earthgod lived was a dank and chilly swamp grown all over with moss, clover, stumpy

水がじめじめしてその表面にはあちこち赤い鉄の渋が湧きあがり見るからどろどろで気味も悪いのでした。

　そのまん中の小さな島のようになったところに丸太で拵えた高さ一間ばかりの土神の祠があったのです。

　土神はその島に帰って来て祠の横に長々と寝そべりました。そして黒い癯せた脚をがりがり掻きました。土神は一羽の鳥が自分の頭の上をまっすぐに翔けて行くのを見ました。すぐ土神は起き直って「しっ。」と叫びました。鳥はびっくりしてよろよろっと落ちそうになりそれからまるではねも何もしびれたようにだんだん低く落ちながら向こうへ遁げて行きました。

　土神は少し笑って起きあがりました。けれども又すぐ向こうの樺の木の立っている高みの方を見るとはっと顔色を変えて棒立ちになりました。それからいかにもむしゃくしゃするという風にそのぼろぼろの髪毛を両手で掻きむしっていました。

　その時谷地の南の方から一人の木樵がやって来ました。三つ森山の方へ稼ぎに出るらしく谷地のふちに沿った細い路を大股に行くのでしたがやっぱり土神のことは知っていたと見えて時々気づかわしそうに土神の祠の方を見ていました。けれども木樵には土神の形は見えなかったのです。

　土神はそれを見るとよろこんでぱっと顔を熱らせました。それから右手をそっちへ突き出して左手でその右手の手首をつかみこっちへ引き寄せるようにしました。すると奇体なことは木樵はみちを歩いていると思いながらだんだん谷地の中に踏み込んで来るようでした。それからびっくりしたように足が早くなり顔も青ざめて口をあいて息をしました。土神は右手のこぶしをゆっくりぐる

reeds, and here and there a thistle or a short, dreadfully twisted willow tree. There were soggy places where the water seeped through in rusty patches. You only had to look at it to tell that it was all muddy and somehow frightening.

On a patch like a small island right in the middle of it stood the earthgod's shrine, which was about six feet high and made of logs.

Back on this island, the earthgod stretched himself out full length on the ground beside his shrine and scratched long and hard at his dark, scraggy legs.

Just then he noticed a bird flying through the sky right above his head, so he sat up straight and shouted "Shoo!" The bird wobbled in alarm and for a moment seemed about to fall, then fled into the distance, gradually losing height as it went, as though its wings were paralyzed.

The earthgod gave a little laugh and was getting to his feet when he happened to glance toward the hillock, not far away, where the birch tree grew. And instantly his rage returned: his face turned pale, his body went as stiff as a poker, and he began tearing at his wild head of hair.

A solitary woodcutter on his way to work on Mt. Mitsumori came up from the south of the hollow, striding along the narrow path that skirted its edge. He seemed to know all about the earthgod, for every now and then he glanced anxiously in the direction of the shrine. But he could not, of course, see anybody there.

When the earthgod caught sight of the woodcutter, he flushed with pleasure. He stretched his arm out toward him, then grasped his own wrist with his other hand and made as though to pull it back. And, strange to say, the woodcutter, who thought he was still walking along the path, found himself gradually moving deeper

っとまわしました。すると木樵はだんだんぐるっと円く
まわって歩いていましたがいよいよひどく周章てだして
まるではあはあはあしながら何べんも同じところを
まわり出しました。何でも早く谷地から遁げて出ようと
するらしいのでしたがあせってもあせっても同じ処を廻
っているばかりなのです。とうとう木樵はおろおろ泣き
出しました。そして両手をあげて走り出したのです。土
神はいかにも嬉しそうににやにやにやにや笑って寝そべ
ったままそれを見ていましたが間もなく木樵がすっかり
逆上せて疲れてばたっと水の中に倒れてしまいますと、
ゆっくりと立ちあがりました。そしてぐちゃぐちゃ大股
にそっちへ歩いて行って倒れている木樵のからだを向こ
うの草はらの方へぽんと投げ出しました。木樵は草の中
にどしりと落ちてううんと言いながら少し動いたようで
したがまだ気がつきませんでした。

土神は大声に笑いました。その声はあやしい波になっ
て空の方へ行きました。

空へ行った声はまもなくそっちからはねかえってガサ
リと樺の木の処にも落ちて行きました。樺の木ははっと
顔いろを変えて日光に青くすきとおりせわしくせわしく
ふるえました。

土神はたまらなそうに両手で髪を掻きむしりながらひ
とりで考えました。おれのこんなに面白くないというの
は第一は狐のためだ。狐のためよりは樺の木のためだ。
狐と樺の木とのためだ。けれども樺の木の方はおれは怒
ってはいないのだ。樺の木を怒らないためにおれはこん
なにつらいのだ。樺の木さえどうでもよければ狐などは
なおさらどうでもいいのだ。おれはいやしいけれどもと
にかく神の分際だ。それに狐のことなどを気にかけなけ

本のタイトルを
お書きください

愛読者カード

ご愛読ありがとうございました。下の項目についてご意見をお聞かせ
頂きたく、ご記入のうえご投函くださいますようお願いいたします。

a　ご住所　　　　　　　　　　　　　〒□□□-□□□□

b　お名前　　　　　　　　　　　　年齢 （　　）歳

　　　　　　　　　　　　　　　　性別　1 男性　2 女性

c　ご職業　1 生徒・学生（小、中、高、大、その他）　2 会社員
　　　　　3 自営（商工、農林漁、サービス、その他）　4 公務員　5 教職員
　　　　　6 自由業（　　　　　　　　）　7 無職（主婦、家事手伝い、その他）
　　　　　8 その他（　　　　　　　　）

d　本書をどこでお知りになりましたか。
　　1 新聞広告（新聞名　　　　　　）　2 雑誌広告（雑誌名　　　　　　）
　　3 書評（書名　　　　　　）　4 実物を見て　5 人にすすめられて
　　6 その他（　　　　　　　　　）

e　どんな本を対訳で読みたいか、お教えください。

f　どんな分野の英語学習書を読みたいか、お教えください。

御協力ありがとうございました。

郵 便 は が き

1 1 2 - 8 7 9 0

料金受取人払

小石川局承認

3565

差出有効期間
平成14年3月
31日まで

東京都文京区音羽一丁目
十七番十四号

講談社 インターナショナル　行
愛読者カード係

|ılıl·ıl·lıllılıllıll·ılıllıllıllıllıllıllıllılı·ıllılıllıll|

★この本についてお気づきの点、ご感想などをお教えください。

and deeper into the hollow. He quickened his pace in alarm, his face turned pale, his mouth opened, and he began to gasp.

Slowly the earthgod twisted his wrist. And as he did so, the woodcutter slowly began to turn in circles. At this he grew more and more alarmed, until finally he was going round and round on the same spot, panting desperately all the while. His one idea seemed to be to get out of the hollow as quickly as he could, but for all his efforts he stayed, circling, where he was. In the end he began to sob and, flinging up his arms, broke into a run.

This seemed to delight the earthgod. He just grinned and watched without getting up from the ground, until before long the woodcutter who by now was giddy and exhausted, collapsed in the, water. Then the earthgod got slowly to his feet. With long strides he squelched his way to where the woodcutter lay and, picking him up, flung him over onto the grassy ground. The woodcutter landed in the grass with a thud. He groaned once and stirred, but still did not come to.

The earthgod laughed loudly. His laughter rose up into the sky in great mysterious waves. Reaching the sky, the sound bounced back down again to the place where the birch tree stood. The birch tree turned suddenly so pale that the sunlight shone green through her leaves, and she began to quiver frantically.

The earthgod tore at his hair with both hands. "It's all because of the fox that I feel so miserable," he told himself. "Or rather, the birch tree. No, the fox and the birch tree. That's why I suffer so much. If only I didn't mind about the tree, I'd mind even less about the fox. I may be nobody much, but I *am* a god after all, and it's

ればならないというのは情けない。それでも気にかかるから仕方ない。樺の木のことなどは忘れてしまえ。ところがどうしても忘れられない。今朝は青ざめて顫えたぞ。あの立派だったこと、どうしても忘れられない。おれはむしゃくしゃまぎれにあんなあわれな人間などをいじめたのだ。けれども仕方ない。誰だってむしゃくしゃしたときは何をするかわからないのだ。

　土神はひとりで切ながってばたばたしました。空を又一疋の鷹が翔けて行きましたが土神はこんどは何とも言わずだまってそれを見ました。

　ずうっとずうっと遠くで騎兵の演習らしいパチパチパチパチ塩のはぜるような鉄砲の音が聞こえました。そらから青びかりがどくどくと野原に流れて来ました。それを呑んだためかさっきの草の中に投げ出された木樵はやっと気がついておずおずと起きあがりしきりにあたりを見廻しました。

　それから俄かに立って一目散に遁げ出しました。三つ森山の方へまるで一目散に遁げました。

　土神はそれを見て又大きな声で笑いました。その声は又青ぞらの方まで行き途中から、バサリと樺の木の方へ落ちました。

　樺の木は又はっと葉の色をかえ見えない位こまかくふるえました。

　土神は自分のほこらのまわりをうろうろうろうろ何べんも歩きまわってからやっと気がしずまったと見えてすっと形を消し融けるようにほこらの中に入って行きました。

disgraceful that I should have to bother myself about a mere fox. But the awful thing is, I do. Why don't I forget all about the birch tree, then? Because I can't. How splendid it was this morning when she went pale and trembled! I was wrong to bully a wretched human being just to work off my temper, but it can't be helped. No one can tell what somebody'll do when he gets really cross."

So dreadfully sad did he feel that he beat at the air in despair. Another bird came flying through the sky, but this time the earthgod just watched it go in silence.

From far, far away came the sound of cavalry at their maneuvers, with a crackling of rifle fire like salt being thrown on flames. From the sky, the blue light poured down in waves. This must have done the woodcutter good, for he came to, sat up timidly, and peered about him. The next moment he was up and running like an arrow shot from a bow. Away he ran in the direction of Mt. Mitsumori.

Watching him, the earthgod gave a great laugh again. Again his laughter soared up to the blue sky and hurtled back down to the birch tree below. Again the tree's leaves went pale and trembled delicately, so delicately that you would scarcely have noticed.

The earthgod walked aimlessly round and round his shrine till finally, when he seemed to feel more settled, he suddenly darted inside.

（四）

　八月のある霧のふかい晩でした。土神は何とも言えずさびしくてそれにむしゃくしゃして仕方ないのでふらっと自分の祠を出ました。足はいつの間にかあの樺の木の方へ向かっていたのです。本当に土神は樺の木のことを考えるとなぜか胸がどきっとするのでした。そして大へんに切なかったのです。このごろは大へんに心持ちが変わってよくなっていたのです。ですからなるべく狐のことなど樺の木のことなど考えたくないと思ったのでしたがどうしてもそれがおもえて仕方ありませんでした。おれはいやしくも神じゃないか、一本の樺の木がおれに何のあたいがあると毎日毎日土神は繰り返して自分で自分に教えました。それでもどうしてもかなしくて仕方なかったのです。殊にちょっとでもあの狐のことを思い出したらまるでからだが灼けるくらい辛かったのです。

　土神はいろいろ深く考え込みながらだんだん樺の木の近くに参りました。そのうちとうとうはっきり自分が樺の木のとこへ行こうとしているのだということに気が付きました。すると俄かに心持ちがおどるようになりました。ずいぶんしばらく行かなかったのだからことによったら樺の木は自分を待っているのかも知れない、どうもそうらしい、そうだとすれば大へんに気の毒だというような考えが強く土神に起こって来ました。土神は草をどしどし踏み胸を踊らせながら大股にあるいて行きました。ところがその強い足なみもいつかよろよろしてしまい土神はまるで頭から青い色のかなしみを浴びてつっ立たなければなりませんでした。それは狐が来ていたのです。もうすっかり夜でしたが、ぼんやり月のあかりに澄んだ霧の向こうから狐の声が聞こえて来るのでした。
「ええ、もちろんそうなんです。器械的に対称の法則に

*

It was a misty night in August. The earthgod was a terribly lonely and so dreadfully cross that he left his shrine on an impulse and started walking. Almost before he realized it, his feet were taking him toward the birch tree. He couldn't say why, but whenever he thought of her, his heart seemed to turn over and he felt intolerably sad. Nowadays he was much easier in his mind than before, and he had done his best not to think about either the fox or the birch tree. But, try as he might, they kept coming into his head. Every day he would tell himself over and over again, "You're a god, after all. What can a mere birch tree mean to you?" But still he felt awfully sad. The memory of the fox, in particular, hurt till it seemed his whole body was on fire.

Wrapped in his own thoughts, the earthgod drew nearer and nearer the birch tree. Finally it dawned on him quite clearly that he was on his way to see her, and his heart began to dance for joy. It had been a long time. She might well have missed him. In fact, the more he thought about it the surer he felt it was so. If this really was the case, then he was very sorry he had neglected her. His heart danced as he strode on through the grass. But before long his stride faltered and he stopped dead; a great blue wave of sadness had suddenly washed over him. The fox was there before him. It was quite dark by now, but he could hear the fox's voice coming through the mist, which was glowing in the vague light of the moon.

"Why, of course," he was saying, "just because something agrees with the laws of symmetry is not to say that it is beautiful. That's nothing more than a dead beauty."

ばかり叶っているからってそれで美しいというわけにはいかないんです。それは死んだ美です。」

「全くそうですわ。」しずかな樺の木の声がしました。

「ほんとうの美はそんな固定した化石した模型のようなもんじゃないんです。対称の法則に叶うって言ったって実は対称の精神を有っているというぐらいのことが望ましいのです。」

「ほんとうにそうだと思いますわ。」樺の木のやさしい声が又しました。土神は今度はまるでべらべらした桃いろの火でからだ中燃やされているようにおもいました。息がせかせかしてほんとうにたまらなくなりました。なにがそんなにおまえを切なくするのか、高が樺の木と狐との野原の中でのみじかい会話ではないか、そんなものに心を乱されてそれでもお前は神と言えるか、土神は自分で自分を責めました。狐が又言いました。

「ですから、どの美学の本にもこれくらいのことは論じてあるんです。」

「美学の方の本沢山おもちですの。」樺の木はたずねました。

「ええ、よけいもありませんがまあ日本語と英語と独乙語のなら大抵ありますね。伊太利のは新しいんですがまだ来ないんです。」

「あなたのお書斎、まあどんなに立派でしょうね。」

「いいえ、まるでちらばってますよ、それに研究室兼用ですからね、あっちの隅には顕微鏡こっちにはロンドンタイムス、大理石のシィザアがころがったりまるっきりごったごたです。」

「まあ、立派だわねえ、ほんとうに立派だわ。」

　ふんと狐の謙遜のような自慢のような息の音がしてしばらくしいんとなりました。

"How right you are," came the birch tree's soft voice.

"True beauty is not something rigid and fossilized. People talk of observing the laws of symmetry, but it's enough so long as the *spirit* of symmetry is present."

"Oh, yes, I'm sure it is," came the birch tree's gentle voice again.

But now the earthgod felt as though red flames were licking his whole body. His breath came in short gasps, and he really thought he couldn't bear it any longer. "What are you so miserable about?" he asked himself crossly. "What is this, after all, but a bit of talk between a birch tree and a fox out in the open country? You call yourself a god, to let things like this upset you?"

But the fox was talking again:

"So all books on art touch on this aspect."

"Do you have many books on art, then?" asked the birch tree.

"Oh, not such an enormous number. I suppose I have most of them in English, German, and Japanese. There's a new one in Italian, but it hasn't come yet."

"What a fine library it must be!"

"No, no. just a few scattered volumes, really. And besides, I use the place for my studies too, so it's rather a mess, what with a microscope in one corner and the London *Times* lying over there, and a marble bust of Caesar here...."

"Oh, but it sounds wonderful! Really wonderful!"

There was a little sniff from the fox that might have been either modesty or pride, then everything was quiet for a while.

By now the earthgod was quite beside himself. From what the fox said, it seemed the fox was actually more

土神はもう居ても立っても居られませんでした。狐の言っているのを聞くと全く狐の方が自分よりはえらいのでした。いやしくも神ではないかと今まで自分で自分に教えていたのが今度はできなくなったのです。ああつらいつらい、もう飛び出して行って狐を一裂きに裂いてやろうか、けれどもそんなことは夢にもおれの考えるべきことじゃない、けれどもそのおれというものは何だ結局狐にも劣ったもんじゃないか、一体おれはどうすればいいのだ、土神は胸をかきむしるようにしてもだえました。

「いつかの望遠鏡まだ来ないんですの。」樺の木がまた言いました。

「ええ、いつかの望遠鏡ですか。まだ来ないんです。なかなか来ないです。欧州航路は大分混乱してますからね。来たらすぐ持って来てお目にかけますよ。土星の環なんかそれぁ美しいんですからね。」

　土神は俄に両手で耳を押さえて一目散に北の方へ走りました。だまっていたら自分が何をするかわからないのが恐ろしくなったのです。

　まるで一目散に走って行きました。息がつづかなくなってばったり倒れたところは三つ森山の麓でした。

　土神は頭の毛をかきむしりながら草をころげまわりました。それから大声で泣きました。その声は時でもない雷のように空へ行って野原中へ聞こえたのです。土神は泣いて泣いて疲れてあけ方ぼんやり自分の祠に戻りました。

(五)

　そのうちとうとう秋になりました。樺の木はまだまっ青でしたがその辺のいのころぐさはもうすっかり黄金いろの穂を出して風に光りところどころすずらんの実も赤く熟しました。

impressive than he was himself. He could no longer console himself with the thought that he was a god if nothing else. It was frightful. He felt like rushing over and tearing the fox in two. He told himself that one should never even think such things. But then, what was he to do? Hadn't he let the fox get the better of him? He clutched at his breast in distress.

"Has the telescope you once mentioned come yet?" started the birch tree again.

"The telescope I mentioned? Oh, no, it hasn't arrived yet. I keep expecting it, but the shipping routes are terribly busy. As soon as it comes, I'll bring it along for you to see. I really must show you the rings around Saturn, for one thing. They're so beautiful."

At this, the earthgod clapped his hands over his ears and fled away toward the north. He had suddenly felt frightened at the thought of what he might do if he stayed there any longer.

He ran on and on in a straight line. When he finally collapsed out of breath, he found himself at the foot of Mt. Mitsumori.

He rolled about in the grass, tearing at his hair. Then he began to cry in a loud voice. The sound rose up into the sky, where it echoed like thunder out of season and made itself heard all over the plain. He wept and wept until dawn, when, tired out, he finally wandered vacantly back to his shrine.

*

Time passed, and autumn came at last. The birch tree was still green, but on the grass round about golden ears had already formed and were glinting in the breeze, and

あるすきとおるように黄金いろの秋の日土神は大へん上機嫌でした。今年の夏からのいろいろなつらい思いが何だかほうっとみんな立派なもやのようなものに変わって頭の上に環になってかかったように思いました。そしてもうあの不思議に意地の悪い性質もどこかへ行ってしまって樺の木なども狐と話したいなら話すがいい、両方ともうれしくてはなすのならほんとうにいいことなんだ、今日はそのことを樺の木に言ってやろうと思いながら土神は心も軽く樺の木の方へ歩いて行きました。

　樺の木は遠くからそれを見ていました。

　そしてやっぱり心配そうにぶるぶるふるえて待ちました。

　土神は進んで行って気軽に挨拶しました。

「樺の木さん。お早う。実にいい天気だな。」

「お早うございます。いいお天気でございます。」

「天道というものはありがたいもんだ。春は赤く夏は白く秋は黄いろく、秋が黄いろになると葡萄は紫になる。実にありがたいもんだ。」

「全くでございます。」

「わしはな、今日は大へんに気ぶんがいいんだ。今年の夏から実にいろいろつらい目にあったのだがやっと今朝からにわかに心持ちが軽くなった。」

　樺の木は返事しようとしましたがなぜかそれが非常に重苦しいことのように思われて返事しかねました。

「わしはいまなら誰のためにでも命をやる。みみずが死ななきゃあならんならそれにもわしはかわってやっていいのだ。」土神は遠くの青いそらを見て言いました。その眼も黒く立派でした。

　樺の木は又何とか返事しようとしましたがやっぱり何か大へん重苦しくてわずか吐息をつくばかりでした。

here and there the berries of lilies of the valley showed ripe and red.

One transparent, golden autumn day found the earthgod in the very best of tempers. All the unpleasant things he had been feeling since the summer seemed somehow to have dissolved into a kind of mist that hovered in only the vaguest of rings over his head. The odd, cross-grained streak in him had quite disappeared, too. He felt that if the birch tree wanted to talk to the fox, well, she could, and that if the two of them enjoyed chatting together, it was a very good thing for them both. He would let the birch tree know how he felt today. With a light heart and his head full of such thoughts, the earthgod set off to visit her.

The birch tree saw him coming in the distance and, as usual, trembled anxiously as she waited for him to arrive.

The earthgod came up and greeted her cheerfully.

"Good morning, Birch Tree. A lovely day we're having!"

"Good morning, Earthgod. Yes, lovely, isn't it?"

"What a blessing the sun is, to be sure! There he is up there, red in the spring, white in the summer, and yellow in the autumn. And when he turns yellow in the autumn, the grapes turn purple. Ah, a blessing indeed!"

"How true."

"D'you know, today I feel much better. I've had all sorts of trials since the summer, but this morning at last something suddenly lifted from my mind."

The birch tree wanted to reply, but for some reason a great weight seemed to be bearing down on her, and she remained silent.

そのときです。狐がやって来たのです。

　狐は土神の居るのを見るとはっと顔いろを変えました。けれども戻るわけにも行かず少しふるえながら樺の木の前に進んで来ました。

「樺の木さん、お早う、そちらに居られるのは土神ですね。」狐は赤革の靴をはき茶いろのレーンコートを着てまだ夏帽子をかぶりながら斯う言いました。

「わしは土神だ。いい天気だ。な。」土神はほんとうに明るい心持ちで斯う言いました。狐は嫉ましさに顔を青くしながら樺の木に言いました。

「お客さまのお出での所にあがって失礼いたしました。これはこの間お約束した本です。それから望遠鏡はいつかはれた晩にお目にかけます。さよなら。」

「まあ、ありがとうございます。」と樺の木が言っているうちに狐はもう土神に挨拶もしないでさっさと戻りはじめました。樺の木はさっと青くなってまた小さくぷりぷり顫えました。

　土神はしばらくの間ただぼんやりと狐を見送って立っていましたがふと狐の赤革の靴のキラッと草に光るのにびっくりして我に返ったと思いましたら俄かに頭がぐらっとしました。狐がいかにも意地をはったように肩をいからせてぐんぐん向こうへ歩いているのです。土神はむらむらっと怒りました。顔も物凄くまっ黒に変わったのです。美学の本だの望遠鏡だのと、畜生、さあ、どうするか見ろ、といきなり狐のあとを追いかけました。樺の木はあわてて枝が一ぺんにがたがたふるえ、狐もそのけはいにどうかしたのかと思って何気なくうしろを見まし

"The way I feel now, I'd willingly die for anybody. I'd even take the place of a worm if it had to die and didn't want to." He gazed far off into the blue sky as he spoke, his eyes dark and splendid.

Again the birch tree wanted to reply, but again something heavy seemed to weigh her down, and she barely managed to sigh.

It was then that the fox appeared.

When the fox saw the earthgod there, he started and turned pale. But he could hardly go back, so, trembling slightly, he went right up to where the birch tree stood.

"Good morning, Birch Tree," said the fox. "I believe that's the earthgod I see there, isn't it?" He was wearing his light brown leather shoes and a brown raincoat and was still in his summer hat.

"Yes, I'm the earthgod. Lovely weather, isn't it?" He spoke without a shadow on his mind.

"I must apologize for coming when you have a visitor," said the fox to the birch tree, his face pale with jealousy. "Here's the book I promised you the other day. Oh, and I'll show you the telescope one evening when the sky's clear. Goodbye."

"Oh, thank you…," began the birch tree, but the fox had already set off toward home without so much as a nod to the other visitor. The birch tree blanched and began to quiver again.

For a while, the earthgod gazed blankly at the fox's retreating form. Then he caught a sudden glint of sunlight on the fox's brown leather shoes amidst the grass, and he came to himself with a start. The next moment, something seemed to click in his brain. The fox was marching steadily into the distance, swaggering almost

たら土神がまるで黒くなって嵐のように追って来るのでした。さあ狐はさっと顔いろを変え口もまがり風のように走って逃げ出しました。

土神はまるでそこら中の草がまっ白な火になって燃えているように思いました。青く光っていたそらさえ俄かにガランとまっ暗な穴になってその底では赤い焔がどうどう音を立てて燃えると思ったのです。

二人はごうごう鳴って汽車のように走りました。
「もうおしまいだ、もうおしまいだ、望遠鏡、望遠鏡、望遠鏡。」と狐は一心に頭の隅のとこで考えながら夢のように走っていました。

向こうに小さな赤剥げの丘がありました。狐はその下の円い穴にはいろうとしてくるっと一つまわりました。それから首を低くしていきなり中へ飛び込もうとして後あしをちらっとあげたときもう土神はうしろからばっと飛びかかっていました。と思うと狐はもう土神にからだをねじられて口を尖らして少し笑ったようになったままぐんにゃりと土神の手の上に首を垂れていたのです。

土神はいきなり狐を地べたに投げつけてぐちゃぐちゃ四五へん踏みつけました。

それからいきなり狐の穴の中にとび込んで行きました。中はがらんとして暗くただ赤土が奇麗に堅められているばかりでした。土神は大きく口をまげてあけながら少し変な気がして外へ出て来ました。

それからぐったり横になっている狐の屍骸のレーンコートのかくしの中に手を入れて見ました。そのかくしの中には茶いろなかもがやの穂が二本はいって居ました。

defiantly as he went. The earthgod began to seethe with rage. His face turned a dreadful dark color. He'd show him what was what, that fox with his art books and his telescopes!

He was up and after him in a flash. The birch tree's branches began to shake all at once in panic. Sensing something wrong, the fox himself glanced around casually, only to see the earthgod, black all over, rushing after him like a hurricane. Off went the fox like the wind, his face white and his mouth twisted with fear.

To the earthgod, the grass about him seemed to be burning like white fire. Even the bright blue sky had suddenly become a yawning black pit with crimson flames burning and roaring in its depths.

They ran snorting and panting like two railway trains. The fox ran as in a dream, and all the while part of his brain kept saving, "This is the end. This is the end. Telescope. Telescope. Telescope."

A small hummock of bare earth lay ahead. The fox dashed around it so as to get to the round hole at its base. He ducked his head, and was diving into the hole, his back legs flicking up as he went, when the earthgod finally pounced on him from behind. The next moment he lay all twisted, with his head drooping over the earthgod's hand and his lips puckered as though smiling slightly.

The earthgod flung the fox down on the ground and stamped one his soft, yielding body four or five times. Then he plunged into the fox's hole. It was quite bare and dark, though the red clay of the floor had been trodden down hard and neat.

The earthgod went outside again, feeling rather strange, with his mouth all slack and crooked. Then he

土神はさっきからあいていた口をそのまままるで途方も
ない声で泣き出しました。

　その泪は雨のように狐に降り狐はいよいよ首をぐんに
ゃりとしてうすら笑ったようになって死んで居たのです。

tried putting a hand inside the pocket of the fox's rain-coat as he lay there limp and lifeless. The pocket contained two brown burrs, the kind foxes comb their fur with. From the earthgod's open mouth came the most extraordinary sound, and he burst into tears.

The tears fell like rain on the fox, and the fox lay there dead, with his head lolling limper and limper and the faintest of smiles on his face.

🍒

オツベルと象
……ある牛飼いがものがたる

第一日曜

オツベルときたら大したもんだ。稲扱器械の六台も据えつけて、のんのんのんのんのんのんと、大そろしない音をたててやっている。

十六人の百姓どもが、顔をまるっきりまっ赤にして足で踏んで器械をまわし、小山のように積まれた稲を片っぱしから扱いて行く。藁はどんどんうしろの方へ投げられて、また新しい山になる。そこらは、籾や藁から発ったこまかな塵で、変にぼうっと黄いろになり、まるで沙漠のけむりのようだ。

そのうすぐらい仕事場で、オツベルは、大きな琥珀のパイプをくわえ、吹殻を藁に落とさないよう、眼を細くして気をつけながら、両手を背中に組みあわせて、ぶらぶら往ったり来たりする。

小屋はずいぶん頑丈で、学校ぐらいもあるのだが、何せ新式稲扱器械が六台もそろってまわってるから、のんのんのんのんふるうのだ。中にはいるとそのために、すっかり腹が空くほどだ。そしてじっさいオツベルは、そいつで上手に腹をへらし、ひるめしどきには、六寸ぐらいのビフテキの、雑巾ほどあるオムレツの、ほくほくしたのをたべるのだ。

とにかく、そうして、のんのんのんのんやっていた。

Ozbel and the Elephant

The First Sunday

Ozbel? Now, there was a fine fellow! He'd installed six threshing machines—six, mind you!—and got them going with a steady *thumpety-thump, thumpety-thump....*

There were sixteen farmhands, all bright red in the face, working the machines with their feet, and a small mountain of cut rice that they were feeding steadily into the machines. The straw was being churned out just as steadily at the back, where it made another, new pile. All around them was a funny yellowish haze from the fine dust rising from the husks and the straw—like a little sandstorm, almost.

Ozbel was strolling up and down in the dim barn with a big amber pipe between his teeth, his hands clasped behind his back, squinting at the pipe to make sure that none of the ash fell on the straw. The barn was quite sturdily built, and big enough for a school. Even so—there being six of those new-fangled threshing machines thumping away all at once—it shook with the vibration. It was enough to make your stomach feel empty when you went inside. And so it was with Ozbel—he'd make himself nice and hungry, then at lunchtime he'd put away a few sizzling hot six-inch steaks or omelettes as big as a man's handkerchief.

Anyway, there they were, all busily thumping away,

そしたらそこへどういうわけか、その、白象がやって来た。白い象だぜ、ペンキを塗ったのでないぜ。どういうわけで来たかって？　そいつは象のことだから、たぶんぶらっと森を出て、ただなにとなく来たのだろう。

　そいつが小屋の入り口に、ゆっくり顔を出したとき、百姓どもはぎょっとした。なぜぎょっとした？　よくきくねえ、何をしだすか知れないじゃないか。かかり合っては大へんだから、どいつもみんな、いっしょうけんめい、じぶんの稲を扱いていた。

　ところがそのときオツベルは、ならんだ器械のうしろの方で、ポケットに手を入れながら、ちらっと鋭く象を見た。それからすばやく下を向き、何でもないというふうで、いままでどおり往ったり来たりしていたもんだ。

　するとこんどは白象が、片脚床にあげたのだ。百姓どもはぎょっとした。それでも仕事が忙しいし、かかり合ってはひどいから、そっちを見ずに、やっぱり稲を扱いていた。

　オツベルは奥のうすぐらいところで両手をポケットから出して、も一度ちらっと象を見た。それからいかにも退屈そうに、わざと大きなあくびをして、両手を頭のうしろに組んで、行ったり来たりやっていた。ところが象が威勢よく、前肢二つつきだして、小屋にあがって来ようとする。百姓どもはぎくっとし、オツベルもすこしぎょっとして、大きな琥珀のパイプから、ふっとけむりをはきだした。それでもやっぱりしらないふうで、ゆっくりそこらをあるいていた。

　そしたらとうとう、象がのこのこ上がって来た。そして器械の前のとこを、呑気にあるきはじめたのだ。

　ところが何せ、器械はひどく廻っていて、籾は夕立か

when what should turn up for some reason but a white elephant.

I mean, a *real* white elephant, not one that somebody had painted white. What was he doing there, you say? Well, being an elephant, I suppose he'd just taken a stroll out of the forest and wandered over. When he slowly put his face in at the entrance to the barn, the farmhands got a shock. I mean, who knows what an elephant mightn't do? But it was safer just to ignore him, so they all went on busily threshing their rice.

Ozbel himself, standing behind the row of machines with his hands in his pockets, just gave a sharp glance at the elephant, then looked down and went on pacing up and down as though nothing had happened.

So this time the white elephant put one foot up onto the raised floor. The farmhands started back. Even so, they had a lot of work to do, and getting involved would have been risky; so, trying not to look at him, they went on threshing.

In the dusky area at the back, Ozbel took his hands out of his pockets and gave the elephant another glance. Then he deliberately gave a big yawn as though he really couldn't have cared less, and clasping his hands behind his head continued walking up and down. But the elephant had got his front legs well forward and was beginning to get up into the barn. The farmhands started in alarm; even Ozbel was a bit shaken, and let out a puff of smoke from his big amber pipe. But he still went on pacing slowly up and down as though he hadn't seen a thing.

So in the end the elephant calmly heaved himself up onto the raised floor. And, cool as you please, he started walking about in the space in front of the machines.

The machines were all working away, though, and chaff

霰のように、パチパチ象にあたるのだ。象はいかにもうるさいらしく、小さなその眼を細めていたが、またよく見ると、たしかに少しわらっていた。

　オツベルはやっと覚悟をきめて、稲扱器械の前に出て、象に話をしようとしたが、そのとき象が、とてもきれいな、鶯みたいないい声で、こんな文句を言ったのだ。

「ああ、だめだ。あんまりせわしく、砂がわしの歯にあたる。」

　まったく籾は、パチパチパチパチ歯にあたり、またまっ白な頭や首にぶっつかる。さあ、オツベルは命懸けだ。パイプを右手にもち直し、度胸を据えて斯う言った。

「どうだい、此処は面白いかい。」

「面白いねえ。」象がからだを斜めにして、眼を細くして返事した。

「ずうっとこっちに居たらどうだい。」

　百姓どもははっとして、息を殺して象を見た。オツベルは言ってしまってから、にわかにがたがた顫え出す。ところが象はけろりとして、

「居てもいいよ。」と答えたもんだ。

「そうか。それではそうしよう。そういうことにしようじゃないか。」オツベルが顔をくしゃくしゃにして、まっ赤になって悦びながらそう言った。

　どうだ、そうしてこの象は、もうオツベルの財産だ。いまに見たまえ、オツベルは、あの白象を、はたらかせるか、サーカス団に売りとばすか、どっちにしても万円以上もうけるぜ。

第二日曜

　オツベルときたら大したもんだ。それにこの前稲扱小

102

was peppering the elephant like hail or a sudden summer shower. This seemed to bother him a bit, because he screwed up his little eyes—though, if you'd looked carefully, you'd have seen he was actually smiling slightly, too.

Finally making up his mind, Ozbel came out in front of the machines to talk to the elephant, but before he could start the elephant spoke up in beautiful, fluty kind of voice:

"Oh, drat this sand—it keeps hitting my tusks."

He was right: the chaff was raining against his tusks, and beating against his white head and neck.

Ozbel decided to take his chance. Switching his pipe to his right hand and plucking up his courage, he said:

"Well? Do you like it here?"

"Oh yes, I do," replied the elephant, leaning to one side and screwing up his eyes.

"How would it be if you stayed on?"

Startled, the farmhands looked at the elephant with bated breath. Ozbel too, now that he had actually got it out, began trembling all over; but the elephant, not a bit put out, said simply:

"I wouldn't mind at all."

"I see. That's fine, then—let's agree on it." As he spoke, his face wrinkled up in a smile and turned bright red with pleasure.

So, what do you think? The white elephant was now Ozbel's property. Was he going to put him to work, or would he sell him off to a circus? Well, I'll tell you one thing, anyway: he wasn't going to lose any money on it—that's for sure!

The Second Sunday
That Ozbel—I can't help admiring him. And the ele-

屋で、うまく自分のものにした、象もじっさい大したもんだ。力も二十馬力もある。第一みかけがまっ白で、牙はぜんたいきれいな象牙でできている。皮も全体、立派で丈夫な象皮なのだ。そしてずいぶんはたらくもんだ。けれどもそんなに稼ぐのも、やっぱり主人が偉いのだ。

「おい、お前は時計は要らないか。」丸太で建てたその象小屋の前に来て、オツベルは琥珀のパイプをくわえ、顔をしかめて斯う訊いた。

「ぼくは時計は要らないよ。」象がわらって返事した。

「まあ持って見ろ、いいもんだ。」斯う言いながらオツベルは、ブリキでこさえた大きな時計を、象の首からぶらさげた。

「なかなかいいね。」象も言う。

「鎖もなくちゃだめだろう。」オツベルときたら、百キロもある鎖をさ、その前肢にくっつけた。

「うん、なかなか鎖はいいね。」三あし歩いて象がいう。

「靴をはいたらどうだろう。」

「ぼくは靴などはかないよ。」

「まあはいてみろ、いいもんだ。」オツベルは顔をしかめながら、赤い張り子の大きな靴を、象のうしろのかかとにはめた。

「なかなかいいね。」象も言う。

「靴に飾りをつけなくちゃ。」オツベルはもう大急ぎで、四百キロある分銅を靴の上から穿め込んだ。

「うん、なかなかいいね。」象は二あし歩いてみて、さもうれしそうにそう言った。

次の日、ブリキの大きな時計と、やくざな紙の靴とはやぶけ、象は鎖と分銅だけで、大よろこびであるいて居った。

「済まないが税金も高いから、今日はすこうし、川から

phant, too—the one he'd so cleverly made his own the other day in the threshing barn—I admire *him*, too, in his own way. He had the strength of twenty horses, for one thing. And his tusks were made of fine ivory. His skin as well was good, strong elephant hide. And he worked hard. Even so, they'd never have made so much if it hadn't been for Ozbel.

"Hey—" he said one day, with his amber pipe in his mouth and his face wrinkling in a smile, standing in front of the elephant house they'd built with logs. "How would you like a watch?"

"I don't need a watch, thank you," replied the elephant with a smile.

"You should have one, just the same. You'll find it very useful," said Ozbel; and he hung a big watch made of tin around his neck.

"It looks all right, doesn't it?" said the elephant.

"I suppose you ought to have a chain, too."

And—would you believe it?—Ozbel fastened a chain weighing a good two hundred pounds to the elephant's front legs.

"Mm—the chain's not half bad, either," said the elephant, taking a few steps on two legs.

"Why don't you wear shoes?"

"What would I do with shoes?"

"Go on, try some—I'm sure you'll like them."

With his face screwed up, Ozbel fitted a pair of big red papier-mâché shoes on the elephant's back feet.

"Not bad at all," said the elephant.

"You need some sort of ornament on them, though."

And quickly Ozbel fixed a weight weighing a good eight hundred pounds to each shoe, as a kind of buckle.

水を汲んでくれ。」オツベルは両手をうしろで組んで、顔をしかめて象に言う。

「ああ、ぼく水を汲んで来よう。もう何ばいでも汲んでやるよ。」

象は眼を細くしてよろこんで、そのひるすぎに五十だけ、川から水を汲んで来た。そして菜っ葉の畑にかけた。

夕方象は小屋に居て、十把の藁をたべながら、西の三日の月を見て、

「ああ、稼ぐのは愉快だねえ、さっぱりするねえ。」と言っていた。

「済まないが税金がまたあがる。今日は少うし森から、たきぎを運んでくれ。」オツベルは房のついた赤い帽子をかぶり、両手をかくしにつっ込んで、次の日象にそう言った。

「ああ、ぼくたきぎを持って来よう。いい天気だねえ。ぼくはぜんたい森へ行くのは大すきなんだ。」象はわらってこう言った。

オツベルは少しぎょっとして、パイプを手からあぶなく落としそうにしたがもうそのときは、象がいかにも愉快なふうで、ゆっくりあるきだしたので、また安心してパイプをくわえ、小さな咳を一つして、百姓どもの仕事の方を見に行った。

そのひるすぎの半日に、象は九百把たきぎを運び、眼を細くしてよろこんだ。

晩方象は小屋に居て、八把の藁をたべながら、西の四日の月を見て、

「ああ、せいせいした。サンタマリア。」と斯うひとりごとしたそうだ。

その次の日だ。

"Yes, they're not bad, I must say," said the elephant, taking a couple of steps and looking rather pleased.

The next day, the big tin watch and the shoddy paper shoes were broken, and the elephant was cheerfully going around with just the chain and buckles on.

"I'm sorry," said Ozbel to the elephant, screwing up his face and clasping his hands behind his back, "but I've got a lot of taxes to pay. I'd like you to go and draw a little water from the river."

"Of course—I'll get you as many buckets as you like."

A smile crinkling his little eyes, the elephant drew fifty buckets of water from the river that morning, and used them to water the vegetables in the fields.

That evening, looking out at the three-day moon in the west as he ate his ten bundles of straw in his shed, the elephant said to himself, "Mm, working for your living is fun, isn't it? You feel so good afterward."

The following day, Ozbel, wearing a red-brimmed hat and with his hands stuck in his pockets, told the elephant:

"I'm sorry, but taxes are going up again. Today I'd like you to fetch a little firewood from the forest."

"Yes, of course," said the elephant with a smile. "The weather's fine, and I love going to the forest."

Ozbel was a bit taken aback; in fact he very nearly dropped his pipe, but the elephant had already set off at a leisurely pace, just as though he really did enjoy it. Relieved, Ozbel stuck the pipe back in his mouth and with a little cough went off to see how the farmhands were getting on.

That afternoon, in just half a day, the elephant, his eyes crinkling with satisfaction, brought back nine hundred bundles of firewood.

「済まないが、税金が五倍になった、今日は少うし鍛冶場へ行って、炭火を吹いてくれないか。」

「ああ、吹いてやろう。本気でやったら、ぼく、もう、息で、石もなげとばせるよ。」

オツベルはまたどきっとしたが、気を落ち付けてわらっていた。

象はのそのそ鍛冶場へ行って、べたんと肢を折って座り、ふいごの代わりに半日炭を吹いたのだ。

その晩、象は象小屋で、七把の藁をたべながら、空の五日の月を見て

「ああつかれたな、うれしいな、サンタマリア」と斯う言った。

どうだ、そうして次の日から、象は朝からかせぐのだ。藁も昨日はただ五把だ。よくまあ、五把の藁などで、あんな力がでるもんだ。

じっさい象はけいざいだよ。それというのもオツベルが、頭がよくてえらいためだ。オツベルときたら大したもんさ。

第五日曜

オツベルかね、そのオツベルは、おれも言おうとしてたんだが、居なくなったよ。

まあ落ちついてきたまえ。前にはなしたあの象を、オツベルはすこしひどくし過ぎた。しかたがだんだんひどくなったから、象はなかなか笑わなくなった。時には赤い竜の眼をして、じっとこんなにオツベルを見おろすようになってきた。

ある晩象は象小屋で、三把の藁をたべながら、十日の月を仰ぎ見て、

The same evening in his shed, as he ate his eight bundles of straw, the elephant looked up at the moon in the west, which was in its fourth day, and said:

"Ah, I feel so good!"

Then, the next day, Ozbel told him:

"I'm sorry, but they've increased our taxes by five times. Today I'd like you to go to the smithy and fan the charcoal fire."

"Of course. Why, if I put my mind to it I could send a rock flying with my breath."

Again Ozbel was a bit startled, but took a grip on himself and smiled.

The elephant lumbered off to the smithy, plumped down, folding his legs under him, and spent half the day acting as a bellows for the charcoal fire.

That evening as he ate his seven bundles of straw in his shed, the elephant looked up at the five-day moon and said:

"Ah, I'm tired. But happy, too."

So, what happened then? From the next day on, the elephant had to start work first thing in the morning. And his straw when he'd got home the day before was just five bundles; you'd wonder how he had all that strength on a miserable five bundles of straw. But elephants are surprisingly economical creatures, you know....

The Fifth Sunday

Ozbel? Oh, Ozbel—I was meaning to tell you, but he's not around any more.

Wait—just be patient and listen! That elephant I was telling you about—well, Ozbel treated him a bit *too* badly. As things gradually got worse, the elephant hardly ever smiled any more, and sometimes he would stare

「苦しいです。サンタマリア。」と言ったということだ。

　こいつを聞いたオッベルは、ことごと象につらくした。

　ある晩、象は象小屋で、ふらふら倒れて地べたに座り、藁もたべずに、十一日の月を見て、

「もう、さようなら、サンタマリア。」と斯う言った。

「おや、何だって？　さよならだ？」月が俄かに象に訊く。

「ええ、さよならです。サンタマリア。」

「何だい、なりばかり大きくて、からっきし意気地のないやつだなあ。仲間へ手紙を書いたらいいや。」月がわらって斯う言った。

「お筆も紙もありませんよう。」象は細うい、きれいな声で、しくしくしくしく泣き出した。

「そら、これでしょう。」すぐ眼の前で、可愛い子どもの声がした。象が頭を上げて見ると、赤い着物の童子が立って、硯と紙を捧げていた。象は早速手紙を書いた。

「ぼくはずいぶん眼にあっている。みんなで出て来て助けてくれ。」

　童子はすぐに手紙をもって、林の方へあるいて行った。

　赤衣の童子が、そうして山に着いたのは、ちょうどひるめしごろだった。このとき山の象どもは、沙羅樹の下のくらがりで、碁などをやっていたのだが、額をあつめてこれを見た。

「ぼくはずいぶん眼にあっている。みんなで出てきて助けてくれ。」

　象は一せいに立ちあがり、まっ黒になって吠えだした。

「オッベルをやっつけよう。」議長の象が高く叫ぶと、

「おう、でかけよう。グララアガア、グララアガア。」みんながいちどに呼応する。

　さあ、もうみんな、嵐のように林の中をつきぬけて、

down steadily at Ozbel with red eyes like a dragon's.

One evening, he looked up at the ten-day moon as he ate his three bundles of straw and said:

"I'm having a hard time."

Ozbel heard him, and was even harder on him than ever.

Then, the following night, the elephant tottered and collapsed on the ground in his shed. Leaving his straw untouched, he looked up at the eleven-day moon and said:

"It's goodbye."

"Eh? What? Good*bye?*" exclaimed the moon.

"Yes, goodbye."

"But you're much too big a fellow to give in like this!" said the moon, laughing. 'You should write a letter to your friends."

"I don't have a writing brush and paper," said the elephant in a faint but beautiful voice. And he began to whimper.

"Here—this is what you want, isn't it?" came a charming child's voice right in front of him. The elephant raised his head and saw a boy in a red robe standing there, holding out an ink block, a writing brush, and paper.

The elephant promptly wrote: "I'm being treated very badly. Please come down from the woods and rescue me."

The boy took the message and immediately headed for the forest.

When he arrived in the hills, it was just lunchtime. The elephants who lived up there were resting in the shade of a bodhi tree, playing chess and so on. They put their heads together to read the letter: "I'm being treated very badly. Please come down from the woods and rescue me."

Rousing themselves, the herd gathered together and

グララアガア、グララアガア、野原の方へとんで行く。どいつもみんなきちがいだ。小さな木などは根こぎになり、藪や何かもめちゃめちゃだ。グヮア　グヮア　グヮアグヮア、花火みたいに野原の中へ飛び出した。それから、何の、走って、走って、とうとう向こうの青くかすんだ野原のはてに、オツベルの邸の黄いろな屋根を見付けると、象はいちどに噴火した。

　グララアガア、グララアガア。その時はちょうど一時半、オツベルは皮の寝台の上でひるねのさかりで、烏の夢を見ていたもんだ。あまり大きな音なので、オツベルの家の百姓どもが、門から少し外へ出て、小手をかざして向こうを見た。林のような象だろう。汽車より速くやってくる。さあ、まるっきり、血の気も失せてかけ込んで、
「旦那あ、象です。押し寄せやした。旦那あ、象です。」と声をかぎりに叫んだもんだ。

　ところがオツベルはやはりえらい。眼をぱっちりとあいたときは、もう何もかもわかっていた。
「おい、象のやつは小屋にいるのか。居る？　居る？居るのか。よし、戸をしめろ。戸をしめるんだよ。早く象小屋の戸をしめるんだ。ようし、早く丸太を持って来い。とじこめちまえ、畜生めじたばたしやがるな、丸太をそこへしばりつけろ。何ができるもんか。わざと力を減らしてあるんだ。ようし、もう五六本持って来い。さあ、大丈夫だとも。あわてるなったら。おい、みんな、こんどは門だ。門をしめろ。かんぬきをかえ。つっぱり。つっぱり。そうだ。おい、みんな心配するなったら。しっかりしろよ。」オツベルはもう仕度ができて、ラッパみたいないい声で、百姓どもをはげました。ところがど

began trumpeting till they were purple in the face.

"We'll let that Ozbel have it!" their leader shouted at the top of his voice.

"Come on—let's go!" the others bellowed.

And in no time they were roaring their way like a hurricane through the woods and toward the open country beyond: furious, every one of them. Small trees and the like were pulled up by the roots, thickets trampled out of recognition. In full cry, they burst onto the plain like rockets. From then on it was run, run, run, till finally in the distance, at the hazy edge of the green countryside, they caught sight of the yellow roof of Ozbel's mansion, and erupted in a frenzy of trumpeting.

It was half past one, and Ozbel was in the middle of a nap on his leather couch, having a dream about ravens. There was such a noise that the farmhands at Ozbel's place went a little way outside the gate and shaded their eyes with their hands to look.

And what did they see but a great wall of elephants, heading straight toward them! They rushed inside and yelled:

"Mr. Ozbel! Elephants! They're coming to attack us! Mr. Ozbel—elephants!"

But Ozbel wasn't a big boss for nothing. The moment his eyes snapped open, he knew exactly what was happening.

"Hey—is that elephant in his shed? He is? Right— shut the door. Shut the *door*! Get the door there closed as soon as you can. Right. Now, quick—go and get some logs. Shut him in. Shut him *in*! Stop flapping about, you idiots! Lash the logs together, across the door. Don't worry—what do you think he can do? I've deliberately

うして、百姓どもは気が気じゃない。こんな主人に巻き添いなんぞ食いたくないから、みんなタオルやはんけちや、よごれたような白いようなものを、ぐるぐる腕に巻きつける。降参をするしるしなのだ。

　オツベルはいよいよやっきとなって、そこらあたりをかけまわる。オツベルの犬も気が立って、火のつくように吠えながら、やしきの中をはせまわる。

　間もなく地面はぐらぐらとゆられ、そこらはばしゃばしゃくらくなり、象はやしきをとりまいた。グララアガア、グララアガア、その恐ろしいさわぎの中から、
「今助けるから安心しろよ。」やさしい声もきこえてくる。
「ありがとう。よく来てくれて、ほんとに僕はうれしいよ。」象小屋からも声がする。さあ、そうすると、まわりの象は、一そうひどく、グララアガア、グララアガア、塀のまわりをぐるぐる走っているらしく、度々中から、怒ってふりまわす鼻も見える。けれども塀はセメントで、中には鉄も入っているから、なかなか象もこわせない。塀の中にはオツベルが、たった一人で叫んでいる。百姓どもは眼もくらみ、そこらをうろうろするだけだ。そのうち外の象どもは、仲間のからだを台にして、いよいよ塀を越しかかる。だんだんにゅうと顔を出す。その皺くちゃで灰いろの、大きな顔を見あげたとき、オツベルの犬は気絶した。さあ、オツベルは射ちだした。六連発のピストルさ。ドーン、グララアガア、ドーン、グララアガア、ドーン、グララアガア、ところが弾丸は通らない、牙にあたればはねかえる。一疋なぞは斯う言った。
「なかなかこいつはうるさいねえ。ばちばち頭へあたるんだ。」

made him weak. Right—get another five or six logs. There—now it's all right. It's all right, I say! Just keep cool. Hey, listen, *listen*—now the gate. Shut the gate! Shoot the bolts! Now put some props against it—props! That's it. Hey—there's nothing to worry about! Nothing at all! Get a grip on yourselves!"

Soon everything was ready, with Ozbel urging them on in ringing tones. But the farmhands, I'm afraid, were scared stiff. They didn't fancy sharing the fate of a boss like him, so they bound their arms around with towels, handkerchiefs, and anything else, however dirty, that looked at all white, as a sign that they were surrendering. Ozbel was rushing around the place more and more frantically. Even his dog got excited and dashed about inside the house, barking fit to burst.

Almost immediately, the earth gave a great shudder, everything turned dark, and the herd of elephants sur-rounded the house, trumpeting fiercely. From out of the dreadful uproar, a gentle voice could be heard saying:

"We'll have you out in a moment, keep calm."

"Thank you," came a voice from the elephant shed. "I'm so glad you're here."

That set the others outside trumpeting still more loudly. They seemed to be running round and round the outer wall, for occasionally a trunk could be seen from inside, waving angrily above it. The wall was made of cement reinforced with iron, so it wasn't easy, even for elephants, to break it down. In the house, Ozbel was the only one shouting; the farmhands hung about uselessly, their minds numb with fright.

Before long, the elephants set about getting over the wall, using each other to stand on. Soon, their heads

オツベルはいつかどっかで、こんな文句をきいたようだと思いながら、ケースを帯からつめかえた。そのうち、象の片脚が、塀からこっちへはみ出した。それからも一つはみ出した。五匹の象が一ぺんに、塀からどっと落ちて来た。オツベルはケースを握ったまま、もうくしゃくしゃに潰れていた。早くも門があいていて、グララアガア、グララアガア、象がどしどしなだれ込む。
「牢はどこだ。」みんなは小屋に押し寄せる。丸太なんぞは、マッチのようにへし折られ、あの白象は大へん瘠せて小屋を出た。
「まあ、よかったね、やせたねえ。」みんなはしずかにそばにより、鎖と分銅をはずしてやった。
「ああ、ありがとう。ほんとにぼくは助かったよ。」白象はさびしくわらってそう言った。

loomed over the top; when Ozbel's dog looked up and saw the great gray wrinkled faces, he fainted right away. Then Ozbel began to fire a six-shooter—*bang, roar! bang, roar! bang, roar!*—but the bullets couldn't penetrate their hides, and just bounced off their tusks.

"Drat these things," said one of the elephants, "they sting!"

"I've heard the same thing said somewhere else, some other time," thought Ozbel, reloading his gun with ammunition from his belt. But then the leg of an elephant suddenly stuck out over the wall. Another followed. And five of them came crashing down at once. In a moment, Ozbel was squashed to a pulp, the pistol's chamber still in his hand. In no time the gate was open, and a wave of trumpeting elephants came pouring in.

"Where's the prison?" they cried.

They descended on the shed. Logs were smashed like so many matches, and the white elephant came out into the open air, a shadow of his old self.

"Thank heavens," they said. "But how *thin* you've got!" They quietly went up to him and removed his chain and weights.

"Yes. Thank you. You've really saved my life," said the white elephant, giving a sad little smile.

毒もみのすきな署長さん

四つのつめたい谷川が、カラコン山の氷河から出て、ごうごう白い泡をはいて、プハラの国にはいるのでした。四つの川はプハラの町で集まって一つの大きなしずかな川になりました。その川はふだんは水もすきとおり、淵には雲や樹の影もうつるのでしたが、一ぺん洪水になると、幅十町もある楊の生えた広い河原が、恐ろしく咆える水で、いっぱいになってしまったのです。けれども水が退きますと、もとのきれいな、白い河原があらわれました。その河原のところどころには、蘆やがまなどの岸に生えた、ほそ長い沼のようなものがありました。

「それは昔の川の流れたあとで、洪水のたびにいくらか形も変わるのでしたが、すっかりなくなるということもありませんでした。その中には魚がたくさん居りました。殊にどじょうとなまずがたくさん居りました。けれどもプハラのひとたちは、どじょうやなまずは、みんなばかにして食べませんでしたから、それはいよいよ増えました。

「なまずのつぎに多いのはやっぱり鯉と鮒でした。それからはやも居りました。ある年などは、そこに恐ろしい大きなちょうざめが、海から遁げて入って来たという、評判などもありました。けれども大人や賢い子供らは、

118

The Police Chief

Four icy mountain streams springing from the glacier on Mt. Karakon roared down in a flurry of white foam into the country of Puhara. At the town of Puhara, the four streams came together to form one large, placid river. The river's waters were usually clear, and clouds and trees were reflected in the still pools that formed along its course. But when the floods came, the broad river flats—a good twenty-five acres, with willow trees growing on them—were filled with fiercely roaring water. Then, once the water receded, the pleasant white flats appeared again.

Here and there on them were what looked like long, narrow ponds, bordered with reeds and bullrushes. These were signs of where the river had flowed in the past; their shape changed somewhat each time there was a flood, but they never disappeared completely. They contained large quantities of fish, particularly loach and catfish, and since the people of Puhara considered these unfit to eat, they went on increasing steadily. Next after catfish in numbers came, as you might expect, carp and roach, but there were dace as well.

One year—rumor had it—a great sturgeon had turned up, having fled there from the sea. But the adults and the brighter of the children dismissed the story with

みんな本当にしないで、笑っていました。第一それを言いだしたのは、剃刀を二梃しかもっていない、下手な床屋のリチキで、すこしもあてにならないのでした。けれどもあんまり小さい子供らは、毎日ちょうざめを見ようとして、そこへ出かけて行きました。いくらまじめに眺めていても、そんな巨きなちょうざめは、泳ぎも浮かびもしませんでしたから、しまいには、リチキは大へん軽べつされました。

さてこの国の第一条の

「火薬を使って鳥をとってはなりません、
　毒もみをして魚をとってはなりません。」

　というその毒もみというのは、何かと言いますと床屋のリチキはこう言う風に教えます。

　山椒の皮を春の午の日の暗夜に剥いて土用を二回かけて乾かしうすでよくつく、その目方一貫匁を天気のいい日にもみじの木を焼いてこしらえた木灰七百匁とまぜる、それを袋に入れて水の中へ手でもみ出すことです。

　そうすると、魚はみんな毒をのんで、口をあぶあぶやりながら、白い腹を上にして浮かびあがるのです。そんなふうにして、水の中で死ぬことは、この国の語ではエップカップと言いました。これはずいぶんいい語です。

　とにかくこの毒もみをするものを押さえるということは警察のいちばん大事な仕事でした。

　ある夏、この町の警察へ、新しい署長さんが来ました。
　この人は、どこか河獺に似ていました。赤ひげがぴんとはねて、歯はみんな銀の入れ歯でした。署長さんは立派な金モールのついた、長い赤いマントを着て、毎日ていねいに町をみまわりました。

a smile. After all, it had started with a barber called Richiki, who had only two razors, was bad at his trade, and was generally unreliable. Even so, the smaller children went there every day for a while in the hope of seeing the newcomer. However solemnly they stared, though, there was no sign of the great fish, either near the surface or swimming down below, so that Richiki ended up the object of great scorn.

Now, Article One of the country's Law states that "It is forbidden to use gunpowder to kill birds, and it is forbidden to use poison bags in order to catch fish," the poison bags in question being described by that same Richiki the barber in the following fashion:

"You peel some *sansho* bark on a dark night on a Day of the Horse in spring, dry it twice in the hot sun, and grind it with a pestle and mortar. With two pounds of this, you mix a pound and a half of wood ash made by burning maple wood on a fine day, put the mixture in a bag, and squeeze it out into the water with your hand."

The fish swallow the poison and float to the surface with their white bellies up and their mouths gasping, a way of dying that is known in the local language as *hepp-kapp*—a most apt expression.

In any case, one of the most important tasks of the Puhara police was to stop people using these poison bags.

One summer, a new chief of police came to the town.

With a red moustache that stuck out stiffly, he somewhat resembled an otter; and his teeth were all capped with silver. As chief of police, he wore a long red cloak with magnificent gold braid, and every day he went around keeping a careful eye on things.

驢馬が頭を下げてると荷物があんまり重過ぎないかと
驢馬追いにたずねましたし家の中で赤ん坊があんまり泣
いていると疱瘡の呪いを早くしないといけないとお母さ
んに教えました。

　ところがそのころどうも規則の第一条を用いないもの
ができてきました。あの河原のあちこちの大きな水たま
りからいっこう魚が釣れなくなって時々は死んで腐った
ものも浮いていました。また春の午の日の夜の間に町の
中にたくさんある山椒の木がたびたびつるりと皮を剥か
れて居りました。けれども署長さんも巡査もそんなこと
があるかなあというふうでした。

　ところがある朝手習いの先生のうちの前の草原で二人
の子供がみんなに囲まれて交る交る話していました。

「署長さんにうんと叱られたぞ。」

「署長さんに叱られたかい。」少し大きなこどもがきき
ました。

「叱られたよ。署長さんの居るのを知らないで石をなげ
たんだよ。するとあの沼の岸に署長さんが誰か三四人と
かくれて毒もみをするものを押さえようとしていたん
だ。」

「何と言って叱られた。」

「誰だ。石を投げるものは。おれたちは第一条の犯人を
押さえようと思って一日ここに居るんだぞ。早く黙って
帰れ。って言った。」

「じゃきっと間もなくつかまるねえ。」

　ところがそれから半年ばかりたちますとまたこどもら
が大さわぎです。

「そいつはもうたしかなんだよ。僕の証拠というのはね、
ゆうべお月さまの出るころ、署長さんが黒い衣だけ着て、

122

If he saw a mule with its head hanging down, he would ask the mule driver if the load wasn't too heavy, and if he heard a baby crying too loudly inside a house, he would tell the mother to perform rites against small-pox before it was too late.

Around that time, though, there were people who began to ignore Article One of the Law. Some of the bigger pools on the river flats ceased to yield any fish at all. Sometimes there were dead fish floating, rotting, on the surface. And very often, after a Day of the Horse in the spring, the *sansho* trees of which the town had many were found stripped clean of their bark during the night. But both the chief and his policemen seemed doubtful whether such things had really happened at all.

One morning, however, two of a group of children standing on the grassy stretch in front of the calligraphy teacher's house were talking to each other:

"I got a good telling-off from the police chief."

"You were told off by the *chief*?" said the other, slightly bigger child.

"I was! I threw a stone. I didn't know anybody was there, but he and three or four other men were hiding on the bank of the pond, trying to catch the people who use poison to catch fish."

"What did he actually say to you?"

"'Who's that, throwing stones?' he said. 'Don't you know we're here all day, on the lookout for the criminal who's breaking Article One? So go away, and keep your mouth shut, too.'"

"Well, it won't be long now before the person's caught, then, will it?" said the other.

頭巾をかぶってね、変な人と話してたんだよ。ね、そら、あの鉄砲打ちの小さな変な人ね、そしてね、『おい、こんどはも少しよく、粉にして来なくちゃいかんぞ。』なんて言ってるだろう。それから鉄砲打ちが何か言ったら、『なんだ、柏の木の皮もまぜて置いた癖に、一俵二両だなんて、あんまり無法なことを言うな。』なんて言ってるだろう。きっと山椒の皮の粉のことだよ。」

　するともう一人が叫びました。

「あっ、そうだ。あのね、署長さんがね、僕のうちから、灰を二俵買ったよ。僕、持って行ったんだ。ね、そら、山椒の粉へまぜるのだろう。」

「そうだ。そうだ。きっとそうだ。」みんなは手を叩いたり、こぶしを握ったりしました。

　床屋のリチキは、商売がはやらないで、ひまなもんですから、あとでこの話をきいて、すぐ勘定しました。

毒もみ収支計算

　　費用の部

　　　　一、金　　二両　山椒皮　一俵

　　　　一、金　　三十銭　灰　一俵

　　　　　　　計　　　二両三十銭也

　　収入の部

　　　　一、金　　十三両　鰻　十三斤

　　　　一、金　　十両　　その他見積もり

　　　　　　　計　　　二十三両也

　　差引勘定

　　　　二十両七十銭　署長利益

In fact, though, half a year passed without anything happening, and the children began making a fuss again:

"Listen. I've got definite proof!" one of them said. "Last night just as the moon was coming up I saw the chief, dressed in a black cloak with a hood over his head, talking to a funny-looking man—I mean, that funny little man who goes hunting with a gun—and he was saying to him, 'Look here—I want it powdered a bit more thoroughly before you bring it along.' Then the hunter said something, and the chief went on: 'What, you charge two taels a bundle even though you mix oak ash with it? Come off it!' I bet they were talking about powdered *sansho* bark!"

At this another of the children shouted, "Hey, I've just remembered! The chief—he bought two bags of ash at our place. I mean, you mix it with the powdered bark, don't you?"

"Yes! That's it!" they shouted, clapping their hands and waving clenched fists. "That's it for sure!"

Richiki the barber, who didn't have many customers and had plenty of time to spare, heard about this later and immediately started calculating:

Balance Sheet for Poison-Bag Fishing

      1. Expenses:

            One bag of bark 2 taels

            One bag of ash   30 mace

            Total   2 taels, 30 mace

      2. Income:

            Thirteen eels   13 taels

            Others (estimated)   10 taels

            Total   23 taels

      3. Police chiefs profit   20 taels, 70 mace

あんまりこんな話がさかんになって、とうとう小さな子供らまでが、巡査を見ると、わざと遠くへ遁げて行って、

「毒もみ巡査、
　なまずはよこせ。」

なんて、力いっぱいからだまで曲げて叫んだりするもんですから、これではとてもいかんというので、プハラの町長さんも仕方なく、家来を六人連れて警察に行って、署長さんに会いました。

　二人が一緒に応接室の椅子にこしかけたとき、署長さんの黄金いろの眼は、どこかずうっと遠くの方を見ていました。

「署長さん、ご存じでしょうか、近頃、林野取締法の第一条をやぶるものが大変あるそうですが、どうしたのでしょう。」

「はあ、そんなことがありますかな。」

「どうもあるそうですよ。わたしの家の山椒の皮もはがれましたし、それに魚が、たびたび死んでうかびあがるというではありませんか。」

　すると署長さんが何だか変にわらいました。けれどもそれも気のせいかしらと、町長さんは思いました。

「はあ、そんな評判がありますかな。」

「ありますとも。どうもそしてその、子供らが、あなたのしわざだと言いますが、困ったもんですな。」

　署長さんは椅子から飛びあがりました。

「そいつは大へんだ。僕の名誉にも関係します。早速犯人をつかまえます。」

「何かおてがかりがありますか。」

「さあ、そうそう、ありますとも。ちゃんと証拠があがっています。」

The talk got so bad that eventually even the small children, when they saw a policeman, would make a great show of running away, then stop and, leaning forward, yell from a distance: "Poison-bag policeman—you might at least let us have the catfish!"

Things got so serious, in fact, that the mayor of Puhara reluctantly took six members of his staff and went to see the chief.

As the two of them sat down side by side on the sofa in the visitors' room, the police chief's golden eyes had a kind of faraway look.

"Chief," said the mayor, "I wonder if you're aware of the talk going around—that someone keeps breaking Article One of the Law? What do you feel about it?"

"Why—is it really true, then?"

"I'm afraid it seems so. The *sansho* tree at my place was stripped of its bark, and they say, you know, that dead fish are often found floating on the water."

At this the chief gave a funny sort of smile. Or perhaps it was just the mayor's imagination?

"Oh, is *that* what people are saying?"

"They certainly are. I'm afraid that ... er ... the children are saying that *you're* responsible. It's rather awkward, isn't it?"

The police chief sprang up from his chair.

"It's awful! It reflects on my honor, for one thing. I will arrest the offender immediately."

"Do you have any clues?"

"Let me think. Yes, of course—I have definite *proof*."

"You know, then ...?"

"Without a shadow of a doubt. You see, the poison bag man is myself!"

「もうおわかりですか。」

「よくわかってます。実は毒もみは私ですがね。」

　署長さんは町長さんの前へ顔をつき出してこの顔を見ろというようにしました。

　町長さんも愕きました。

「あなた？　やっぱりそうでしたか。」

「そうです。」

「そんならもうたしかですね。」

「たしかですとも。」

　署長さんは落ち着いて、卓子の上の鐘を一つカーンと叩いて、赤ひげのもじゃもじゃ生えた、第一等の探偵を呼びました。

　さて署長さんは縛られて、裁判にかかり死刑ということにきまりました。

　いよいよ巨きな曲がった刀で、首を落とされるとき、署長さんは笑って言いました。

「ああ、面白かった。おれはもう、毒もみのことときたら、全く夢中なんだ。いよいよこんどは、地獄で毒もみをやるかな。」

　みんなはすっかり感服しました。

And the police chief turned his face toward the mayor as though to say, take a good look. The mayor was startled.

"You? So it was you, after all?"

"That's right."

"You're quite sure, then?"

"Absolutely."

And calmly clanging the bell that stood on the table, the chief summoned a senior detective with a bushy red beard.

Thus it was that the police chief came to be tied up, put on trial, and sentenced to death.

Just as the great curved sword was about to lop off his head, the chief smiled and said:

"Well, it was fun! As far as I'm concerned, I'd be happy doing nothing but catch fish with poison bags all day. And now I think, perhaps, I'll try it in hell."

They were all immensely impressed.

鹿踊りのはじまり

　そのとき西のぎらぎらのちぢれた雲のあいだから、夕陽は赤くななめに苔の野原に注ぎ、すすきはみんな白い火のようにゆれて光りました。わたくしが疲れてそこに睡りますと、ざあざあ吹いていた風が、だんだん人のことばにきこえ、やがてそれは、いま北上の山の方や、野原に行われていた鹿踊りの、ほんとうの精神を語りました。

　そこらがまだまるっきり、丈高い草や黒い林のままだったとき、嘉十はおじいさんたちと北上川の東から移ってきて、小さな畑を開いて、粟や稗をつくっていました。

　あるとき嘉十は、栗の木から落ちて、少し左の膝を悪くしました。そんなときみんなはいつでも、西の山の中の湯の湧くとこへ行って、小屋をかけて泊まって療すのでした。

　天気のいい日に、嘉十も出かけて行きました。糧と味噌と鍋とをしょって、もう銀いろの穂を出したすすきの野原をすこしびっこをひきながら、ゆっくりゆっくり歩いて行ったのです。

　いくつもの小流れや石原を越えて、山脈のかたちも大きくはっきりなり、山の木も一本一本、すぎごけのように見わけられるところまで来たときは、太陽はもうよほど西に外れて、十本ばかりの青いはんのきの木立の上に、少し青ざめてぎらぎら光ってかかりました。

The First Deer Dance

From a gap in the ragged, gleaming clouds to the west, the red rays of the setting sun slanted down on the mossy plain, and the swaying fronds of pampas grass shone like white fire. I was tired, and lay down to sleep. Gradually, the rustling of the breeze began to sound to my ears like human speech, and before long it was telling me the true meaning of the Deer Dance that the countryfolk still perform in the hills and on the plain of Kitakami.

Long ago, in the days when the area was still covered with tall grass and black forests, Kaju, together with his grandfather and the others, came to live there from somewhere east of the river Kitakami. They settled there, cleared the land, and began growing millet.

One day, Kaju fell out of a chestnut tree and hurt his left knee a little. At such times, it was the local custom to go to the mountains in the west where there was a hot spring, build a shelter there, and bathe in the spring until one was cured.

One fine morning, then, Kaju set out for the spring. With his dumplings, his bean paste, and his pot on his back, he walked slowly, limping slightly as he went, across the open country where the plumes of pampas grass were blowing silver.

嘉十は芝草の上に、せなかの荷物をどっかりおろして、栃と粟とのだんごを出して喰べはじめました。すすきは幾むらも幾むらも、はては野原いっぱいのように、まっ白に光って波をたてました。嘉十はだんごをたべながら、すすきの中から黒くまっすぐに立っている、はんのきの幹をじつにりっぱだとおもいました。

　ところがあんまり一生けん命あるいたあとは、どうもなんだかお腹がいっぱいのような気がするのです。そこで嘉十も、おしまいに栃の団子をとちの実のくらい残しました。

「こいづば鹿さ呉でやべか。それ、鹿、来て喰。」と嘉十はひとりごとのように言って、それをうめばちそうの白い花の下に置きました。それから荷物をまたしよって、ゆっくりゆっくり歩きだしました。

　ところが少し行ったとき、嘉十はさっきのやすんだところに、手拭を忘れて来たのに気がつきましたので、急いでまた引っ返しました。あのはんのきの黒い木立がじき近くに見えていて、そこまで戻るぐらい、なんの事でもないようでした。

　けれども嘉十はぴたりとたちどまってしまいました。

　それはたしかに鹿のけはいがしたのです。

　鹿が少なくても五六疋、湿っぽいはなづらをずうっと延ばして、しずかに歩いているらしいのでした。

　嘉十はすすきに触れないように気を付けながら、爪立てをして、そっと苔を踏んでそっちの方へ行きました。

　たしかに鹿はさっきの栃の団子にやってきたのでした。

「はあ、鹿等あ、すぐに来たもな。」と嘉十は咽喉の中で、笑いながらつぶやきました。そしてからだをかがめ

On he went, over streams and across stony wastes, till the mountain range loomed large and clear and he could pick out each single tree on the mountains like the pins in a pincushion. By now the sun was far gone in the west and glittered palely just above the tops of a stand of a dozen alder trees.

Kaju set the load on his back down on the grass, took out some chestnut-and-millet dumplings, and began to eat. The pampas grass stretched away from him in tuft after tuft—so many of them that they seemed to ripple in shining white waves all over the plain. As he ate his dumplings, Kaju thought to himself what a fine sight the trunks of the alders made, rising perfectly straight up out of the high grass.

But it had been such a hard walk he was almost too tired to eat. He was soon full, and in the end, despite himself, he had to leave a piece of dumpling about the size of a chestnut burr.

"I'll leave 'er for the deer," he said to himself. "Deer, do 'ee come and eat!" And he put it down by a small white flower that grew at his feet. Then he shouldered his pack and slowly, quite slowly, set off again.

But he had only gone a short way when he realized that he had left his cotton towel at the place where he'd stopped to rest, so he turned back again in a hurry. He could still see the dark stand of alder trees quite close, so to go back was really not much trouble. Yet before he reached the place, he suddenly stopped quite still, sensing beyond all doubt that the deer were already there.

And there, indeed, they were—at least five or six of them, walking toward something, with their moist noses stretched out far in front of them. Kaju tiptoed over the

て、そろりそろりと、そっちに近よって行きました。

　一むらのすすきの陰から、嘉十はちょっと顔をだして、びっくりしてまたひっ込めました。六疋ばかりの鹿が、さっきの芝原を、ぐるぐるぐるぐる環になって廻っているのでした。嘉十はすすきの隙間から、息をこらしてのぞきました。

　太陽が、ちょうど一本のはんのきの頂にかかっていましたので、その梢はあやしく青くひかり、まるで鹿の群れを見おろしてじっと立っている青いいきもののようにおもわれました。すすきの穂も、一本ずつ銀いろにかがやき、鹿の毛並みがことにその日はりっぱでした。

　嘉十はよろこんで、そっと片膝をついてそれに見とれました。

　鹿は大きな環をつくって、ぐるくるぐるくる廻っていましたが、よく見るとどの鹿も環のまんなかの方に気がとられているようでした。その証拠には、頭も耳も眼もみんなそっちへ向いて、おまけにたびたび、いかにも引っぱられるように、よろよろと二足三足、環からはなれてそっちへ寄って行きそうにするのでした。

　もちろん、その環のまんなかには、さっきの嘉十の栃の団子がひとかけ置いてあったのでしたが、鹿どものしきりに気にかけているのは決して団子ではなくて、そのとなりの草の上にくの字になって落ちている、嘉十の白い手拭らしいのでした。嘉十は痛い足をそっと手で曲げて、苔の上にきちんと座りました。

　鹿のめぐりはだんだんゆるやかになり、みんなは交る交る、前肢を一本環の中の方へ出して、今にもかけ出して行きそうにしては、びっくりしたようにまた引っ込めて、とっとっとっとっしずかに走るのでした。その足音は気もちよく野原の黒土の底の方までひびきました。そ

moss toward them, taking care not to brush against the pampas grass.

No mistake about it, the deer had come for the dumpling he had left. "Hah, deer bain't wasting no time," he muttered to himself with a smile and, bending down low, crept slowly in their direction.

He peeped out from behind a clump of pampas grass, then drew back in surprise. Six deer were walking round and round in a ring on the stretch of turf. Hardly daring to breathe, Kaju peered at them from between the pampas stems.

The sun had touched the summit of one of the alder trees, and its topmost branches shone with a strange green light, so that it looked for all the world like some green living creature standing stock-still, gazing down at the deer. Each plume of pampas grass shone separate and silver, and the deer's coats seemed even glossier than usual. Delighted, Kaju gently lowered himself onto one knee and concentrated on watching them.

They were moving in a wide circle, and he soon noticed that every one of them seemed intent on something that lay in the center of the ring. He was sure of it, because their heads and eyes and ears were all pointing in that direction. What was more, from time to time one or the other of them would break the circle and stagger a few paces inward as though drawn toward the center.

In the middle of the ring, of course, was the chestnut dumpling that Kaju had left there a while ago. The thing that was bothering the deer so much, though, was not the dumpling, it seemed, but Kaju's white cotton towel, which lay in a curve where it had fallen on the ground. Bending his bad leg gently with one hand, Kaju

れから鹿どもはまわるのをやめてみんな手拭のこちらの方に来て立ちました。

　嘉十はにわかに耳がきいんと鳴りました。そしてがたがたふるえました。鹿どもの風にゆれる草穂のような気もちが、波になって伝わって来たのでした。

　嘉十はほんとうにじぶんの耳を疑いました。それは鹿のことばがきこえてきたからです。

「じゃ、おれ行って見で来べが。」

「うんにゃ、危ないじゃ。も少し見でべ。」

　こんなことばもきこえました。

「何時だがの狐みだいに口発破などさ罹ってあ、つまらないもな、高で栃の団子などでよ。」

「そだそだ、全ぐだ。」

　こんなことばも聞きました。

「生ぎものだがも知れないじゃい。」

「うん。生ぎものらしどごもあるな。」

　こんなことばも聞こえました。そのうちにとうとう一疋が、いかにも決心したらしく、せなかをまっすぐにして環からはなれて、まんなかの方に進み出ました。

　みんなは停まってそれを見ています。

　進んで行った鹿は、首をあらんかぎり延ばし、四本の脚を引きしめ引きしめそろりそろりと手拭に近づいて行きましたが、俄かにひどく飛びあがって、一目散に遁げ戻ってきました。廻りの五疋も一ぺんにぱっと四方へちらけようとしましたが、はじめの鹿が、ぴたりととまりましたのでやっと安心して、のそのそ戻ってその鹿の前に集まりました。

「なじょだた。なにだた、あの白い長いやづあ。」

「縦に皺の寄ったもんだけぁな。」

sat himself neatly on his heels on the moss in order to watch.

Gradually the deer's circling slowed down. Now they moved at a gentle trot, every so often dropping out of the ring and putting one foreleg forward toward the center as though about to break into a run, then just as soon drawing back again and trotting on once more. Their hooves thudded pleasantly on the dark soil of the plain. Finally, they stopped circling altogether and came and stood in a group between Kaju and the towel.

Without warning, Kaju's ears began to ring and his body to shake: a feeling as of grass swaying in the breeze—the same thing that the deer were feeling—was coming to him in waves. And the next moment, though he could scarcely credit his own senses, he could actually hear the deer talking.

"Shall I go for to look, then?" one was saying.

"Naw, 'er be dangerous. Better watch 'er a bit longer."

"Mustn't get caught by no trick like old Fox did. 'Er be only for a dumpling, when all's said and done."

"Right, right. Only too right."

So went the deers' talk.

"'Er may be alive."

"Aye, 'er be summat like a living crittur, indeed."

In the end one of them seemed to make up his mind. He straightened his back, left the group, and stepped forward. All the other deer stopped to watch.

Inch by inch, he edged toward the towel with his neck stretched out just as far as it would go and his legs all bunched up beneath him. Then, quite suddenly, he shot up in the air and came flying back like an arrow.

「そだら生ぎものだないがべ、やっぱり蕈などだべが。毒蕈だべ。」

「うんにゃ。きのごだない。やっぱり生ぎものらし。」

「そうが。生ぎもので皺うんと寄ってらば、年老りだな。」

「うん年老りの番兵だ。ううははは。」

「ふふふ青白の番兵だ。」

「ううははは、青じろ番兵だ。」

「こんどおれ行って見べが。」

「行ってみろ、大丈夫だ。」

「喰っつがないが。」

「うんにゃ、大丈夫だ。」

　そこでまた一疋が、そろりそろりと進んで行きました。五疋はこちらで、ことりことりとあたまを振ってそれを見ていました。

　進んで行った一疋は、たびたびもうこわくて、たまらないというように、四本の脚を集めてせなかを円くしたりそっとまたのばしたりして、そろりそろりと進みました。

　そしてとうとう手拭のひと足こっちまで行って、あらんかぎり首を延ばしてふんふん嗅いでいましたが、俄かにはねあがって遁げてきました。みんなもびくっとして一ぺんに遁げだそうとしましたが、その一ぴきがぴたりと停まりましたのでやっと安心して五つの頭をその一つの頭に集めました。

「なじょだた、なして逃げで来た。」

「嚙じるべとしたようだたもさ。」

「ぜんたいなにだけぁ。」

「わがらないな。とにかぐ白どそれがら青ど、両方のぶちだ。」

138

The other five deer scattered in all four directions, but the first deer stopped dead when he got back to where he'd started, so they calmed down and, sheepishly returning, gathered in front of him.

"How were 'er? What do 'er be? That long white thing?"

"'Er do have wrinkles all the way down 'er."

"Then 'er bain't a living crittur. 'Er be a toadstool or something, after all! Poisonous too, I don't doubt."

"Naw, 'er bain't no toadstool. 'Er be a living thing, all right."

"Be 'er, now! Alive and lots of wrinkles too—'er be getting on in years, then."

"Aye, that sentry guarding the dumpling be a very *elderly* sentry. Oh, ho-ho-ho-ho!"

"Eh, he-he-he-he! A blue and white sentry!"

"Oh, ho-ho-ho-ho! Private Blue-'n-White."

"Shall *I* go for to look now?"

"Do 'ee go now. 'Er be safe enough."

"'Er won't bite, will 'er?"

"Naw, 'er be safe, I'd say."

So another deer crept forward. The five who stayed behind nodded their heads approvingly as they watched.

The deer who had gone forward seemed scared to death. Time and time again he bunched his four legs up and arched his back ready for flight, only to stretch them out gingerly and creep on again.

At last he reached a spot only a step away from the towel. He stretched his neck out just as far as it would go and went *sniff, sniff,* at the towel, then suddenly leapt up in the air and came dashing back. They all gave a start and began to run off, but the second deer stopped dead

「匂ぁなじょだ、匂ぁ。」

「柳の葉みだいな匂だな。」

「はでな、息吐でるが、息。」

「さあ、そでば、気付けないがた。」

「こんどぁ、おれぁ行って見べが。」

「行ってみろ。」

　三番目の鹿がまたそろりそろりと進みました。そのときちょっと風が吹いて手拭がちらっと動きましたので、その進んで行った鹿はびっくりして立ちどまってしまい、こっちのみんなもびくっとしました。けれども鹿はやっとまた気を落ちつけたらしく、またそろりそろりと進んで、とうとう手拭まで鼻さきを延ばした。

　こっちでは五匹がみんなことりことりとお互いにうなずき合って居りました。そのとき俄かに進んで行った鹿が竿立ちになって躍りあがって遁げてきました。

「何して遁げできた。」

「気味悪ぐなてよ。」

「息吐でるが。」

「さあ、息の音ぁ為ないがけぁな。口も無いようだけあな。」

「あだまあるが。」

「あだまもゆぐわがらないがったな。」

「そだらこんだおれ行って見べが。」

　四番目の鹿が出て行きました。これもやっぱりびくびくものです。それでもすっかり手拭の前まで行って、いかにも思い切ったらしく、ちょっと鼻を手拭に押しつけて、それから急いで引っ込めて、一目さんに帰ってきました。

「おう、柔っけもんだぞ。」

「泥のようにが。」

as soon as he got back, so they took courage and gathered their faces close about his head.

"How were 'er? Why did 'ee run away?"

"Rut I thought 'er were going to bite me!"

"What can 'er be, now?"

"No telling. What be sure is that 'er be white and blue, in patches, like."

"How do 'er smell? Eh?"

"'Er do smell like willow leaves."

"Do 'er breathe?"

"I didn't rightly notice that."

"Shall *I* go now?"

"Aye, do 'ee go now.

The third deer cautiously advanced. Just then a slight breeze stirred the towel. He stopped in his tracks in fright, and the others gave a violent start. After a while, though, he seemed to calm down, and inched forward again until at last he could stretch the tip of his nose out to the towel.

The five deer left behind were nodding at each other knowingly. But just then the deer out in front went quite stiff, shot up in the air, and came racing back.

"What did 'ee run away for?"

"'Cause I had a strange feeling, like."

"Be 'er breathing?"

"Well, I don't rightly think I heard 'er *breathing*. 'Er don't seem to have no mouth, either."

"Do 'er have a head?"

"I couldn't rightly tell about that, either."

"Then shall *I* go and see this time?"

The fourth deer set out. He was really just as scared as the rest, but he went all the way up to the towel and, ever

「うんにゃ。」

「草のようにが。」

「うんにゃ。」

「ごまざいの毛のようにが。」

「うん、あれよりぁ、も少し硬ぱしな。」

「なにだべ。」

「とにかぐ生ぎもんだ。」

「やっぱりそうだが。」

「うん、汗臭いも。」

「おれも一遍行ってみべが。」

　五番目の鹿がまたそろりそろりと進んで行きました。この鹿はよほどおどけもののようでした。手拭の上にすっかり頭をさげて、それからいかにも不審だというように、頭をかくっと動かしましたので、こっちの五疋がはねあがって笑いました。

　向こうの一疋はそこで得意になって、舌を出して手拭を一つべろりと嘗めましたが、にわかに怖くなったとみえて、大きく口をあけて舌をぶらさげて、まるで風のように飛んで帰ってきました。みんなもひどく愕きました。

「じゃ、じゃ、噛じらえだが、痛ぐしたが。」

「プルルルルル。」

「舌抜がれだが。」

「プルルルルル。」

「なにした、なにした。なにした。じゃ。」

「ふう、ああ、舌縮まってしまったたよ。」

「なじょな味だた。」

「味無いがたな。」

「生ぎもんだべが。」

「なじょだが判らない。こんどぁ汝ぁ行ってみろ。」

「お。」

142

so boldly, pressed his nose right against it. Then he drew back in a hurry and scampered straight toward them.

"Ah, 'er be soft."

"Like mud, would'er be?"

"Naw."

"Like the fur on bean pods?"

"Mm—summat harder than that."

"What could 'er be, then?"

"Any rate, 'er be a living crittur."

"'Ee reckon so, after all?"

"Aye, 'er be *sweaty*."

"I think I'll go and have a look meself."

The fifth deer in turn crept slowly forward. This one seemed to be something of a joker, for he dangled his nose right over the towel, then gave his head a great jerk as much as to say, "Now this looks very suspicious." The other five deer skipped about with amusement.

This encouraged the deer out in front, and he gave the towel a great lick. But then he, too, was suddenly seized with fright and came darting back, with his mouth open and his tongue lolling out. The others were dreadfully alarmed.

"Were 'ee bitten, then? Did 'er hurt?"

But he just shivered and shivered.

"Has yer tongue come loose, then?"

Still he shivered and shivered.

"Now, what be up with 'ee? C'mon, speak up!"

"Phew! Ah! Me tongue be all numb, like!"

"What kind of taste do 'er have?"

"No taste."

"Would 'er be alive?"

"I don't rightly know. Do 'ee go and have a look now."

"Aye."

おしまいの一疋がまたそろそろ出て行きました。みんながおもしろそうに、ことこと頭を振って見ていますと、進んで行った一疋は、しばらく首をさげて手拭を嗅いでいましたが、もう心配もなにもないという風で、いきなりそれをくわえて戻ってきました。そこで鹿はみなぴょんぴょん飛びあがりました。
「おう、うまい、うまい、そいづさい取ってしめば、あどは何っても怖っかなぐない。」
「きっともて、こいづぁ大きな蝸牛の旱からびだのだな。」
「さあ、いいが、おれ歌うだらはんてみんな廻れ。」
　その鹿はみんなのなかにはいってうたいだし、みんなはぐるぐるぐるぐる手拭をまわりはじめました。

「のはらのまん中の	めっけもの
すっこんすっこの	栃だんご
栃のだんごは	結構だが
となりにいからだ	ふんながす
青じろ番兵は	気にかかる。
青じろ番兵は	ふんにゃふにゃ
吠えるもさないば	泣ぐもさない
痩せで長くて	ぶぢぶぢで
どごが口だが	あだまだが
ひでりあがりの	なめぐじら。」

　走りながら廻りながら踊りながら、鹿はたびたび風のように進んで、手拭を角でついたり足でふんだりしました。嘉十の手拭はかあいそうに泥がついてところどころ穴さえあきました。
　そこで鹿のめぐりはだんだんゆるやかになりました。
「おう、こんだ団子お食ばがりだじょ。」
「おう、煮だ団子だじょ。」
「おう、まん円けじょ。」

Slowly, the last deer went forward. The others all watched, nodding their heads with interest as he bent down and sniffed at the thing for a while. Then, quite suddenly, he picked it up in his mouth and came back with it as though there was nothing at all to be afraid of any more. The other deer bounced up and down with delight.

"Well done! Well done! Once we've got 'er, bain't nothing to be afeared of!"

"For sure, 'er be just a big dried-up slug."

"C'mon now, I'll sing, so do 'ee all dance around 'er."

The deer who had said this went into the middle of the group and began to sing, and the rest began to circle round and round the towel.

They ran and whirled and danced, and again and again as they did so one or the other of them would dash forward and stab the towel with his antlers or trample it with his hooves. In no time, Kaju's poor towel was all muddy and holed. Then gradually the deer's circling slowed down.

"Ah, *now* for the dumpling!"

"Ah, a boiled dumpling 'n all!"

"Ah, 'er be quite round!"

"Ah, *yum yum*!"

"Ah, luvly!"

The deer split up and gathered about the chestnut dumpling. Then they all ate one mouthful of it in turn, beginning with the deer who had gone up to the towel first. The sixth and last deer got a piece hardly bigger than a bean.

Then they formed a ring again and began walking round and round. Kaju had been watching the deer so intently that he almost felt he himself was one of them.

「おう、はんぐはぐ。」

「おう、すっこんすっこ。」

「おう、けっこ。」

　鹿はそれからみんなばらばらになって、四方から栃の
だんごを囲んで集まりました。

　そしていちばんはじめに手拭に進んだ鹿から、一口ず
つ団子をたべました。六疋めの鹿は、やっと豆粒のくら
いをたべただけです。

　鹿はそれからまた環になって、ぐるぐるぐるぐるめぐ
りあるきました。

　嘉十はもうあんまりよく鹿を見ましたので、じぶんま
でが鹿のような気がして、いまにもとび出そうとしまし
たが、じぶんの大きな手がすぐ眼にはいりましたので、
やっぱりだめだとおもいながらまた息をこらしました。

　太陽はこのとき、ちょうどはんのきの梢の中ほどにか
かって、少し黄いろにかがやいて居りました。鹿のめぐ
りはまただんだんゆるやかになって、たがいにせわしく
うなずき合い、やがて一列に太陽に向いて、それを拝む
ようにしてまっすぐに立ったのでした。嘉十はもうほん
とうに夢のようにそれに見とれていたのです。

　一ばん右はじにたった鹿が細い声でうたいました。

「はんの木の
　　みどりみじんの葉の向さ
　　じゃらんじゃらランの
　　お日さん懸がる。」

　その水晶の笛のような声に、嘉十は目をつぶってふる
えあがりました。右から二ばん目の鹿が、俄かにとびあ
がって、それからからだを波のようにうねらせながら、
みんなの間を縫ってはせまわり、たびたび太陽の方にあ
たまをさげました。それからじぶんのところに戻るやぴ

146

He was on the point of rushing out to join them, when he caught sight of his own large, clumsy hand; so he gave up the idea, and went on trying to keep his breathing quiet.

Now the sun had reached the middle branches of the alder tree and was shining with a yellowish light. The deer's dance grew slower and slower. They started nodding to each other busily, and soon drew themselves up in a line facing the sun, standing perfectly straight as though in homage to it. Kaju watched in a dream, forgetful of everything else. All at once, the deer at the right-hand end of the line began to sing in a high, thin voice.

> See the setting sun decline,
> Blazing out behind the leaves
> That delicately shine
> Green upon the alder tree.

Kaju shut his eyes and shivered all over at the sound of the voice, which was like a crystal flute.

Then the second deer from the right suddenly leapt up and, twisting his body to and fro, ran in and out between the others, bowing his head again and again to the sun till at last he returned to his own place, stopped quite still, and began to sing.

> Now the sun's behind its back,
> See the leafy alder tree
> Like a mirror crack
> And shatter in a million lights.

Kaju caught his breath and himself bowed low to the

たりととまってうたいました。
「お日さんを
　　せながさしょえば　はんの<ruby>木<rt>ぎ</rt></ruby>も
　　くだげで光る
　　<ruby>鉄<rt>てつ</rt></ruby>のかんがみ。」
　はあと<ruby>嘉十<rt>かじゅう</rt></ruby>もこっちでその立派な太陽とはんのきを<ruby>拝<rt>おが</rt></ruby>みました。右から三ばん目の鹿は首をせわしくあげたり下げたりしてうたいました。
「お日さんは
　　はんの<ruby>木<rt>ぎ</rt></ruby>の<ruby>向<rt>もご</rt></ruby>さ、<ruby>降<rt>ふ</rt></ruby>りでても
　　すすぎ、ぎんがぎが
　　まぶしまんぶし。」
　ほんとうにすすきはみんな、まっ白な火のように<ruby>燃<rt>も</rt></ruby>えたのです。
「ぎんがぎがの
　　すすぎの<ruby>中<rt>なが</rt></ruby>さ立ぢあがる
　　はんの<ruby>木<rt>ぎ</rt></ruby>のすねの
　　<ruby>長<rt>な</rt></ruby>んがい、かげぼうし。」
　五番目の鹿がひくく首を<ruby>垂<rt>た</rt></ruby>れて、もうつぶやくようにうたいだしていました。
「ぎんがぎがの
　　すすぎの<ruby>底<rt>そご</rt></ruby>の<ruby>日暮<rt>ひぐ</rt></ruby>れかだ
　　<ruby>苔<rt>こげ</rt></ruby>の野はらを
　　<ruby>蟻<rt>あり</rt></ruby>こも行がず。」
　このとき鹿はみな首を垂れていましたが、六番目が<ruby>俄<rt>にわ</rt></ruby>かに首をりんとあげてうたいました。
「ぎんがぎがの
　　すすぎの<ruby>底<rt>そご</rt></ruby>でそっこりと
　　咲ぐうめばぢの
　　<ruby>愛<rt>え</rt></ruby>どしおえどし。」

148

sun in its glory, and to the alder tree. Now the third deer from the right began to sing, bending and raising his head all the while.

Homeward though the sun may go,
Down beyond the alder tree,
See the grass aglow,
Dazzling white across the plain.

It was true—the pampas grass was all ablaze, like a sea of white fire.

Long and black the shadow lies
On the shimmering pampas grass
Where against the skies
Straight and tall the alder grows.

Now the fifth deer hung his head low and started singing in a voice that was hardly more than a murmur.

See, the sun is sinking low
In the shimmering pampas grass.
Ants now homeward go
Through the moss upon the plain.

Soon all the deer were hanging their heads. But suddenly the sixth deer raised his head proudly and sang:

Shy white flower, content to pass
Your quiet days where none can see
Amidst the autumn grass—
Of all, the loveliest to me.

鹿はそれからみんな、みじかく笛のように鳴いてはね
あがり、はげしくはげしくまわりました。
　北から冷たい風が来て、ひゅうと鳴り、はんの木はほ
んとうに砕けた鉄の鏡のようにかがやき、かちんかちん
と葉と葉がすれあって音をたてたようにさえおもわれ、
すすきの穂までが鹿にまじって一しょにぐるぐるめぐっ
ているように見えました。
　嘉十はもうまったくじぶんと鹿とのちがいを忘れて、
「ホウ、やれ、やれい。」と叫びながらすすきのかげか
ら飛び出しました。
　鹿はおどろいて一度に竿のように立ちあがり、それか
らはやてに吹かれた木の葉のように、からだを斜めにし
て逃げ出しました。銀のすすきの波をわけ、かがやく
夕陽の流れをみだしてはるかにはるかに遁げて行き、そ
のとおったあとのすすきは静かな湖の水脈のようにいつ
までもぎらぎら光って居りました。
　そこで嘉十はちょっとにが笑いをしながら、泥のつい
て穴のあいた手拭をひろってじぶんもまた西の方へある
きはじめたのです。
　それから、そうそう、苔の野原の夕陽の中で、わたくし
はこのはなしをすきとおった秋の風から聞いたのです。

Then all the deer together gave a short, sharp call like the cry of a flute, leapt up in the air, and began to dash round and round in a ring.

A cold wind came whistling from the north. The alder tree sparkled as though it really were a broken mirror. Its leaves actually seemed to tinkle as they brushed against each other, and the plumes of grass seemed to be spinning around with the deer.

By now Kaju had forgotten all about the difference between himself and the deer. "Ho! Bravo, bravo!" he cried, and rushed out from his hiding place.

For a moment the deer stopped stiff and straight in alarm, then they were fleeing like leaves before a gale. Their bodies bent forward in haste, breasting the waves of silver grass and the shining sunset, they fled far, far into the distance, leaving the pampas grass where they had passed glittering on and on, like the wake of a boat on a quiet lake.

Kaju smiled a rueful smile. Then he picked up his muddy, torn towel and set off toward the west.

And that was all, until I heard the story from the clear autumn breeze in the late sunlight that day on the mossy plain.

❦

祭の晩

山の神の秋の祭りの晩でした。
亮二はあたらしい水色のしごきをしめて、それに十五銭もらって、お旅屋にでかけました。「空気獣」という見世物が大繁盛でした。

それは、髪を長くして、だぶだぶのずぼんをはいたあばたな男が、小屋の幕の前に立って、「さあ、みんな、入れ入れ。」と大威張りでどなっているのでした。亮二が思わず看板の近くまで行きましたら、いきなりその男が、

「おい、あんこ、早ぐ入れ。銭は戻りでいいから。」と亮二に叫びました。亮二は思わず、つっと木戸口を入ってしまいました。すると小屋の中には、高木の甲助だの、だいぶ知っている人たちが、みんなおかしいようなまじめなような顔をして、まん中の台の上を見ているのでした。台の上に空気獣がねばりついていたのです。それは大きな平べったいふらふらした白いもので、どこが頭だか口だかわからず、口上言いがこっち側から棒でつっつくと、そこは引っこんで向うがふくれ、向うをつつくとこっちがふくれ、まん中を突くとまわりが一たいふくれました。亮二は見っともないので、急いで外へ出ようとしましたら、土間の窪みに下駄がはいってあぶなく倒れそうになり、隣の頑丈そうな大きな男にひどくぶっ

Night of the Festival

It was the night of the festival of the mountain god.

Wearing his new light-blue sash and armed with fifteen pennies that his mother had given him as pocket money, Ryoji set off for the place where the portable shrine had been installed. One of the sideshows set up nearby was called "The Air Beast" and was doing a roaring trade, he'd heard.

A man wearing baggy trousers, with long hair and a pockmarked face, was standing in front of the curtain of the booth. "Come one, come all!" he boomed. "Come and see the show!" Ryoji happened to be glancing idly at the placard, so the man called out to him: "Hey, kid, come on in! You can pay on the way out."

Almost without thinking, Ryoji found himself drawn in through the entrance. Inside, he found Kosuke and quite a number of other people he knew, all staring with half-amused, half-serious expressions at something displayed on a platform in the center.

Clinging to the top of the stand was the air beast. It was big and flattish and wobbly and white, with no particular head or mouth. When the showman poked it with a stick, it gave way on this side and swelled out on the other side, and when he poked it on the other side it came out on this side, and when he poked it in the middle it

つかりました。びっくりして見上げましたら、それは古い白縞の単物に、へんな簔のようなものを着た、顔の骨ばって赤い男で、向こうも愕いたように亮二を見おろしていました。その眼はまん円で煤けたような黄金いろでした。亮二が不思議がってしげしげ見ていましたら、にわかにその男が、眼をぱちぱちっとして、それから急いで向こうを向いて木戸口の方に出ました。亮二もついて行きました。その男は木戸口で、堅く握っていた大きな右手をひらいて、十銭の銀貨を出しました。亮二も同じような銀貨を木戸番にわたして外へ出ましたら、従兄の達二に会いました。その男の広い肩はみんなの中に見えなくなってしまいました。

　達二はその見世物の看板を指さしながら、声をひそめて言いました。

「お前はこの見世物にはいったのかい。こいつはね、空気獣だなんて言ってるが、実はね、牛の胃袋に空気をつめたものだそうだよ。こんなものにはいるなんて、おまえはばかだな。」

　亮二がぽんやりそのおかしな形の空気獣の看板を見ているうちに、達二が又言いました。

「おいらは、まだおみこしさんを拝んでいないんだ。あした又会うぜ。」そして片脚で、ぴょんぴょん跳ねて、人ごみの中にはいってしまいました。

　亮二も急いでそこをはなれました。その辺一ぱいにならんだ屋台の青い苹果や葡萄が、アセチレンのあかりできらきら光っていました。

　亮二は、アセチレンの火は青くてきれいだけれどもどうも大蛇のような悪い臭いがある、などと思いながら、そこを通り抜けました。

　向こうの神楽殿には、ぽんやり五つばかりの提灯がつ

swelled out all round. Ryoji didn't like it at all, and was getting out as quickly as he could when his wooden clog caught in a hole in the bare earth. He nearly fell over, and collided heavily with the tall, solid-looking person next to him. Looking up in surprise, he saw a man with a red, heavy-boned face, wearing an old white- striped summer kimono and a peculiar garment resembling a shaggy straw cape over his shoulders. The man looked down at him, just as startled as he was. His eyes were perfectly round and a kind of smoky gold in color.

Ryoji was still staring at him when all of a sudden the man blinked his eyes rapidly, turned away, and made in a hurry for the exit. Ryoji went after him. On the way out, the man opened his large right hand, which had been tightly clenched, and produced a ten-penny silver coin. Ryoji took out a similar coin, gave it to the person waiting to be paid, and went outside, only to bump into his cousin Tatsuji. The man's broad shoulders disappeared into the crowd.

"Did you go into that show?" asked Tatsuji in a low voice, pointing at the placard. "They call it an air beast, but people say it's really just a cow's stomach full of air. I think you're stupid to pay to see something like that."

Ryoji was still staring vacantly at the placard with its oddly shaped creature when Tatsuji said, "I haven't had a look at the portable shrine yet. See you tomorrow." And he went off into the crowd, hopping on one leg.

Ryoji, too, quickly moved away. The green apples and grapes piled on the rows of stalls that lined both sides gleamed in the light of the acetylene lamps.

He walked on between them, thinking to himself vaguely that the blue flames of the lamps were pretty but

いて、これからおかぐらがはじまるところらしく、てびらがねだけしずかに鳴って居りました。（昌一もあのかぐらに出る）と亮二は思いながら、しばらくぼんやりそこに立っていました。

そしたら向こうのひのきの陰の暗い掛茶屋の方で、なにか大きな声がして、みんながそっちへ走って行きました。亮二も急いでかけて行って、みんなの横からのぞき込みました。するとさっきの大きな男が、髪をもじゃもじゃして、しきりに村の若い者にいじめられているのでした。額から汗を流してなんべんも頭を下げていました。

何か言おうとするのでしたが、どうもひどくどもってしまって語が出ないようすでした。

てかてか髪をわけた村の若者が、みんなが見ているので、いよいよ勢いよくどなっていました。

「貴様みたいな、他処から来たものに馬鹿にされて堪っか。早く銭を払え、銭を。無いのか、この野郎。無いなら何して物食った。こら。」

男はひどくあわてて、どもりながらやっと言いました。

「た、た、た、薪百把持って来てやるがら。」

掛茶屋の主人は、耳が少し悪いと見えて、それをよく聞きとりかねて、却って大声で言いました。

「何だと。たった二串だと。あたりまえさ。団子の二串やそこら、呉れてやってもいいのだが、おれはどうもきさまの物言いが気に食わないのでな。やい。何つうつらだ。こら、貴さん。」

男は汗を拭きながら、やっと又言いました。

「薪をあとで百把持って来てやっから、許して呉れろ。」

すると若者が怒ってしまいました。

「うそをつけ、この野郎。どこの国に、団子二串に薪百把払うやづがあっか。全体きさんどこのやつだ。」

156

gave off an unpleasant smell, like a dragon's breath.

Over in the enclosure they used for the festival dance, five paper lanterns cast a dim light. It seemed that the dance was about to begin, as a small cymbal was sounding quietly. Ryoji hung about there for a while, remembering that his friend Shoichi was due to appear in it.

Just then he heard loud voices from the direction of the refreshment stalls that stood in the dark shadow of some cypress trees, and everybody started running in that direction. Ryoji hurried over with the rest and peered around the sides of the grown-ups.

The big man he'd seen a while ago was standing there, his hair all disheveled, being bullied by some young men from the village. The sweat was running down his forehead as he bowed to them again and again. He was trying to say something, but stuttered so badly that he couldn't get the words out.

One young fellow with a neat parting in his sleek hair was gradually shouting louder and louder because he knew people were watching.

"Oh no you don't—no outsider pulls a trick like that. Come on, where's your money? You don't have any, eh? Then why did you eat them? Eh?"

The man was in a terrible state and barely managed to stammer, "I'll b-b-b-bring you a hundred bundles of firewood instead."

The fellow running the tea stall seemed to be slightly deaf, for his voice got even louder still:

"What's that—only a couple of dumplings, you say? What do you expect? I'd let you have 'em free, but I don't like the way you talk. Yes, you!"

Wiping away the sweat, the man just managed again

「そ、そ、そ、そ、そいつはとても言われない。許して呉れろ。」男は黄金色の眼をぱちぱちさせて、汗をふきふき言いました。一緒に涙もふいたようでした。

「ぶん撲れ、ぶん撲れ。」誰かが叫びました。

亮二はすっかりわかりました。

（ははあ、あんまり腹がすいて、それにさっき空気獣で十銭払ったので、あともう銭のないのも忘れて、団子を食ってしまったのだな。泣いている。悪い人でない。却って正直な人なんだ。よし、僕が助けてやろう。）

亮二はこっそりがま口から、ただ一枚残った白銅を出して、それを堅く握って、知らないふりをしてみんなを押しわけて、その男のそばまで行きました。男は首を垂れ、手をきちんと膝まで下げて、一生けん命口の中で何かもにゃもにゃ言っていました。

亮二はしゃがんで、その男の草履をはいた大きな足の上に、だまって白銅を置きました。すると男はびっくりした様子で、じっと亮二の顔を見下していましたが、やがていきなり屈んでそれを取るやいなや、主人の前の台にぱちっと置いて、大きな声で叫びました。

「そら、銭を出すぞ。これで許して呉れろ。薪を百把あとで返すぞ。栗を八斗あとで返すぞ。」言うが早いか、いきなり若者やみんなをつき退けて、風のように外へ遁げ出してしまいました。

「山男だ、山男だ。」みんなは叫んで、がやがやあとを追おうとしましたが、もうどこへ行ったか、影もかたちも見えませんでした。

風がごうごうっと吹き出し、まっくろなひのきがゆれ、掛茶屋のすだれは飛び、あちこちのあかりは消えました。

かぐらの笛がそのときはじまりました。けれども亮二はもうそっちへは行かないで、ひとり田圃の中のほの白

to get out, "I'll b-bring you a hundred bundles of fire-wood ... so let me go."

That made the other burst out: "You rotten liar! Who'd hand over all that firewood for two dumplings? Where're you from, anyway?"

"Th-th-th-th-that's something I just can't tell you. Let me go now." The man was blinking his golden eyes and wiping furiously at the sweat. He seemed to be wiping away some tears as well.

"Beat him up! Come on, beat him up!" someone shouted.

Suddenly, Ryoji understood everything. "I know—" he thought, "he got terribly hungry, and he'd paid to see the air beast, then he went and ate the dumplings forgetting he hadn't got any money left. He's crying. He's not a bad man. Just the opposite—he's too honest. Right. I'm going to help him out."

Stealthily he took from his purse the one remaining coin, clutched it tightly in his hand, and, pushing his way through the crowd as unobtrusively as possible, went up to the man. The man was hanging his head, with his hands resting humbly on his knees, furiously mumbling something.

Ryoji crouched down and, without saying anything, placed the nickel coin on top of the man's big foot in its straw sandal.

The man gave a start and stared down into Ryoji's face, then swiftly bent down, took up the coin, and slammed it on the counter of the stall, shouting:

"There, there's your money! Now let me go. I'll bring the firewood later. And four bushels of chestnuts." No sooner had he said this than he thrust the people surrounding him aside and fled like the wind.

い路を、急いで家の方へ帰りました。早くお爺さんに山男の話を聞かせたかったのです。ぼんやりしたすばるの星がもうよほど高くのぼっていました。

　家に帰って、廐の前から入って行きますと、お爺さんはたった一人、いろりに火を焚いて枝豆をゆでていましたので、亮二は急いでその向こう側に座って、さっきのことをみんな話しました。お爺さんははじめはだまって亮二の顔を見ながら聞いていましたが、おしまいとうとう笑い出してしまいました。

　「ははあ、そいつは山男だ。山男というものは、ごく正直なもんだ。おれも霧のふかい時、度々山で遭ったことがある。しかし山男が祭りを見に来たことは今度はじめてだろう。はっはっは。いや、いままでも来ていても見付からなかったのかな。」

　「おじいさん、山男は山で何をしているのだろう。」

　「そうさ、木の枝で狐わなをこさえたりしてるそうだ。こういう太い木を一本、ずうっと曲げて、それをもう一本の枝でやっと押さえて置いて、その先へ魚などぶら下げて、狐だの熊だの取りに来ると、枝にあたってばちんとはねかえって殺すようにしかけたりしているそうだ。」

　その時、表の方で、どしんがらがらがらっと言う大きな音がして、家は地震の時のようにゆれました。亮二は思わずお爺さんにすがりつきました。お爺さんも少し顔色を変えて、急いでランプを持って外に出ました。

　亮二もついて行きました。ランプは風のためにすぐに消えてしまいました。

　その代わり、東の黒い山から大きな十八日の月が静かに登って来たのです。

　見ると家の前の広場には、太い薪が山のように投げ出

"It's a wild man. A wild man of the hills!" they all cried and ran after him, chattering to each other excitedly; but he'd already disappeared without a trace.

The wind suddenly howled, the great black cedars swayed, the bamboo curtains at the tea stall flew up, and lights blew out here and there.

Just then the flute began to play for the festival dance, but instead of going to watch it Ryoji hurried home along the dim white paths between the paddy fields. He was in a hurry to tell his grandfather about the wild man of the hills. Already the Pleiades was shining dimly quite high up in the sky.

Back at home he went in past the stable and found his grandfather all alone, cooking some soybeans over a fire in the open hearth. Ryoji quickly sat down opposite him and told him everything that had happened. At first his grandfather listened quietly, watching the boy's face as he talked, but when he got to the end he burst out laughing.

"Oh yes," he laughed, "that's a wild man of the hills, all right. The wild men are very honest. I've often met them up in the hills myself on misty days. But I'm sure no one's ever heard of one coming to see a festival before." He laughed again. "Or maybe they've come before and nobody's noticed, eh?"

"Grandpa, what do they do up there?"

"Well, they say they make fox traps, for one thing, using the branches of trees. They bend down a branch as thick as this and hold it down with another branch, then they dangle a fish or something from the end so that when a fox or bear comes to eat it, the branch springs up again and kills it."

されてありました。太い根や枝までついた、ぼりぼりに折られた太い薪でした。お爺さんはしばらく呆れたように、それをながめていましたが、俄かに手を叩いて笑いました。

「はっはっは、山男が薪をお前に持って来て呉れたのだ。俺はまたさっきの団子屋にやるという事だろうと思っていた。山男もずいぶん賢いもんだな。」

亮二は薪をよく見ようとして、一足そっちへ進みましたが、忽ち何かに滑ってころびました。見るとそこらいちめん、きらきらきらきらする栗の実でした。亮二は起きあがって叫びました。

「おじいさん、山男は栗も持って来たよ。」

お爺さんもびっくりして言いました。

「栗まで持って来たのか。こんなに貰うわけには行かない。今度何か山へ持って行って置いて来よう。一番着物がよかろうな。」

亮二はなんだか、山男がかあいそうで泣きたいようなへんな気もちになりました。

「おじいさん、山男はあんまり正直でかあいそうだ。僕何かいいものをやりたいな。」

「うん、今度夜具を一枚持って行ってやろう。山男は夜具を綿入れの代わりに着るかも知れない。それから団子も持って行こう。」

亮二は叫びました。

「着物と団子だけじゃつまらない。もっともっといいものをやりたいな。山男が嬉しがって泣いてぐるぐるはねまわって、それからからだが天に飛んでしまう位いいものをやりたいなあ。」

おじいさんは消えたランプを取りあげて、

「うん、そういういいものあればなあ。さあ、うちへ入

Just then there was a great thud and rattling outside, and the whole house shook as in an earthquake. Ryoji found himself clinging tightly to his grandfather. The old man, who had gone rather pale himself, hurried outside with a lamp.

Ryoji followed after him. The lamp blew out almost immediately, but it didn't matter, for the moon in its eighteenth day was rising silently over the dark hills to the east.

And there, in the open space in front of the house, a great pile of thick faggots lay flung down on the ground. They were massive pieces, roughly broken, with thick roots and branches still attached to them. His grandfather gazed at them for a while in astonishment, then suddenly clapped his hands together and laughed.

"The wild man of the hills has brought *you* some firewood. And there I was thinking he was going to give it to the fellow at the festival. The wild man knows what he's up to!"

Ryoji was stepping forward to get a better look at the firewood when suddenly he slipped on something and fell over. Looking closer, he found the ground was strewn with shiny chestnuts.

"Grandpa!" he shouted, getting up again. "The man brought chestnuts too!"

"Well! So he even remembered them," said his grandfather in astonishment. "We can't possibly accept all this. Next time I go into the hills, I'll take along something and leave it for him. I expect he'd like something to wear best of all."

Suddenly Ryoji had a funny feeling, as though he wanted to cry.

って豆をたべろ。そのうちにおとうさんも隣から帰るから。」と言いながら、家の中にはいりました。

　亮二はだまって青い斜めなお月さまをながめました。

　風が山の方で、ごうっと鳴って居ります。

"Grandpa, I feel sorry for him. He's too honest, isn't he? I'd like to give him something nice.

"Yes. Next time, perhaps, I'll take him a quilted coat. A wild man might prefer a thick, quilted coat to a thin, padded one for the winter. And I'll take him some dumplings."

"But that's not enough—just clothes and dumplings!" shouted Ryoji. "I want to give him something that'll make him cry and dance about the place for joy, something so nice he'll think he's in heaven."

His grandfather picked up the unlit lamp.

"Mm. That's if we can *find* such a thing," he said. "Come on, then, let's go indoors and have the beans. Your father'll be back from next door before long." And he led the way inside.

Ryoji said nothing but looked up at the pale blue, lopsided moon.

The wind was roaring in the hills.

セロ弾きのゴーシュ

　ゴーシュは町の活動写真館でセロを弾く係りでした。けれどもあんまりじょうずでないという評判でした。じょうずでないどころではなく、実は仲間の楽手のなかではいちばんへたでしたから、いつでも楽長にいじめられるのでした。

　ひるすぎみんなは楽屋にまるくならんで今度の町の音楽会へ出す第六交響曲の練習をしていました。

　トランペットは一生けん命歌っています。

　クラリネットもボーボーとそれに手伝っています。

　ヴァイオリンも二いろ風のように鳴っています。

　ゴーシュも口をりんと結んで眼を皿のようにして楽譜を見つめながらもう一心に弾いています。

　にわかに、ぱたっと楽長が両手を鳴らしました。

　みんなぴたりと曲をやめてしんとしました。楽長がどなりました。

　「セロがおくれた。トォテテ　テテテイ、ここからやり直し。はいっ。」みんなは今の所の少し前の所からやり直しました。ゴーシュは顔をまっ赤にして額に汗を出しながら、やっといま言われたところを通りました。ほっと安心しながら、つづけて弾いていますと楽長がまた手をぱっと拍ちました。

　「セロっ。糸が合わない。困るなあ。ぼくはきみにドレ

166

Gorsch the Cellist

Gorsch was the man who played the cello at the moving-picture theater in town. Unfortunately, he had a reputation for being none too good a player. "None too good," perhaps, was hardly the word, for if the truth be told, he was worse than any of his fellow musicians and was forever being bullied by the conductor for that reason.

One afternoon they were all sitting in a circle backstage rehearsing the Sixth Symphony, which they were soon to perform at the town's concert hall.

The trumpets were blaring for all they were worth.

The clarinets were tootling away in support.

The violins, too, were playing like fury.

Gorsch was scraping away with the rest of them, oblivious to everything else, his lips pressed tight together and his eyes as big as saucers as he stared at the score in front of him.

All of a sudden the conductor clapped his hands.

They all stopped playing instantly, and silence fell.

"The cello was late!" shouted the conductor. "*Tum-tiddy, tiddy-tee*—take it again from the bit that goes *tum-tiddy, tiddy-tee*. Right?" So they started again from a point just before where they had got to. With his face red and his forehead all sweaty Gorsch managed somehow to get safely past the tricky bit. And he was playing

ミファを教えてまでいるひまはないんだがなあ。」

　みんなはきのどくそうにして、わざとじぶんの譜をのぞき込んだりじぶんの楽器をはじいてみたりしています。ゴーシュはあわてて糸を直しました。これはじつはゴーシュも悪いのですがセロもずいぶん悪いのでした。

「今の前の小節から。はいっ。」

　みんなはまたはじめました。ゴーシュも口をまげて一生けん命です。そしてこんどはかなり進みました。いいあんばいだと思っていると楽長がおどすような形をしてまたぱたっと手を拍ちました。またかとゴーシュはどきっとしました。が、ありがたいことにはこんどは別の人でした。ゴーシュはそこでさっきのじぶんのときみんながしたようにわざとじぶんの譜へ眼を近づけて何か考えるふりをしていました。

「ではすぐ今の次。はいっ。」

　そらと思って弾きだしたかと思うと、いきなり楽長が足をどんと踏んでどなりだしました。

「だめだ。まるでなっていない。このへんは曲の心臓なんだ。それがこんながさがさしたことで。諸君。演奏までもうあと十日しかないんだよ。音楽を専門にやっているぼくらがあの金沓鍛冶だの砂糖屋の丁稚なんかの寄り集まりに負けてしまったら、いったいわれわれの面目はどうなるんだ。おいゴーシュ君。君には困るんだがなあ。表情ということがまるでできてない。怒るも喜ぶも感情というものがさっぱり出ないんだ。それにどうしてもぴたっとほかの楽器と合わないもんなあ。いつでもきみだけとけた靴のひもを引きずってみんなのあとをついてあるくようなんだ。困るよ、しっかりしてくれないとねえ。光輝あるわが金星音楽団がきみ一人のために悪評をとるようなことでは、みんなへもまったくきのどくだからな。

the next part with a feeling of relief when, once again, the conductor clapped his hands.

"Cello! You're off pitch! Whatever *are* we to do with you? I just haven't got time to teach you the simple scale, you know!"

The others looked sorry for Gorsch and deliberately peered at their scores or set about tuning their instruments. Hastily, Gorsch tightened his strings.

"From the previous bar. Right!"

They all began again. Gorsch's mouth was twisted with the effort to play properly. For once, they managed to get quite far without any trouble, and he was just feeling rather pleased with himself when the conductor scowled and brought things to a halt. "Oh no—not again," thought Gorsch, with a lurch of his heart. But this time, luckily, it was someone else. So Gorsch deliberately peered closely at his music, as the others had done for him just now, and did his best to look engrossed in something else.

"Let's go straight on to the next bit. Right!"

But Gorsch, feeling smug, had no sooner started playing than the conductor gave a great stamp of his foot and started shouting.

"It won't do. You're all at sixes and sevens. This part's the heart of the whole work, and look what a hash you're making of it. Gentlemen, we've got just ten days till the performance. We're professional musicians—how can we look people in the eye if we do no better than any old bunch of scrapers and blowers? You, Gorsch. You're one of the main problems. You just don't have any *expression*. No anger, no joy—no feeling at all. And you don't keep in perfect time with the other instruments, either. You always drag along behind with

では今日は練習はここまで、休んで六時にはかっきりボックスへはいってくれたまえ。」

　みんなはおじぎをして、それからたばこをくわえてマッチをすったりどこかへ出て行ったりしました。

　ゴーシュはそのそまつな箱みたいなセロをかかえて壁の方へ向いて口をまげてほろぼろ泪をこぼしましたが、気をとり直してじぶんだけたったひとり、いまやったところをはじめからしずかに、もいちど弾きはじめました。

　その晩おそくゴーシュは何か巨きな黒いものをしょってじぶんの家へ帰ってきました。家といってもそれは町はずれの川ばたにあるこわれた水車小屋で、ゴーシュはそこにたった一人ですんでいて午前は小屋のまわりの小さな畑でトマトの枝をきったり甘藍の虫をひろったりして、ひるすぎになるといつも出て行っていたのです。ゴーシュがうちへはいってさっきの黒い包みをあけました。それはなんでもない。あの夕方のごつごつしたセロでした。ゴーシュはそれを床の上にそっと置くと、いきなり棚からコップをとってバケツの水をごくごくのみました。

　それから頭を一つふって椅子へかけるとまるで虎みたいな勢いでひるの譜を弾きはじめました。

　譜をめくりながら弾いては考え考えては弾き、しまいまで行くとまたはじめからなんべんもなんべんも、ごうごうごうごう弾きつづけました。

　夜中もとうにすぎて、しまいはもうじぶんが弾いているのかもわからないようになって、顔もまっ赤になり眼もまるで血走ってとてもものすごい顔つきになり、いまにも倒れるかと思うように見えました。

　そのとき誰かうしろの扉をとんとんとたたくものがありました。

your shoelaces dangling. It won't do—you must pull yourself together. It's not fair to the others to let the name of the Venus Orchestra be dragged in the mud all because of one man. Well, then—that's enough rehearsing for now. Have a rest and be in the pit at six sharp."

They all bowed, then reached for cigarettes or wandered off outside.

With his cheap, boxlike cello held in his arms, Gorsch turned to face the wall. His mouth twisted and great tears rolled down his cheeks, but he soon pulled himself together and, all by himself, began to play again from the beginning, very softly, the part they had just done.

Late that evening, Gorsch arrived home carrying an enormous black object on his back. His home was really no more than a tumbledown old millhouse standing by the river on the outskirts of the town. He lived there all alone. His mornings he spent thinning out the tomatoes in the small field surrounding the mill and picking grubs off the cabbages, but in the afternoon he always went out.

Gorsch went indoors and opened the black bundle. It was, of course, the ugly great cello he'd been playing earlier that evening. He lowered it gently to the floor, then took a glass and gulped down some water out of a bucket.

Then, giving a shake of his head, he sat down on a chair and began to play the piece of music they'd rehearsed that day, attacking his instrument with all the ferocity of a tiger.

Turning over the pages of the score, he played a while and thought, thought a while and played, and when he got to the end he started again from the beginning, rumbling his way through the same thing over and over again.

「ホーシュ君か」ゴーシュはねぼけたように叫びました。ところがすうと扉を押してはいって来たのはいままで五、六ぺん見たことのある大きな三毛猫でした。

　ゴーシュの畑からとった半分熟したトマトをさも重そうに持って来てゴーシュの前におろして言いました。

「ああくたびれた。なかなか運搬はひどいやな。」

「なんだと。」ゴーシュがききました。

「これおみやげです。たべてください。」三毛猫が言いました。

　ゴーシュはひるからのむしゃくしゃを一ぺんにどなりつけました。

「誰がきさまにトマトなど持ってこいと言った。第一おれがきさまらのもってきたものなど食うか。それからそのトマトだっておれの畑のやつだ。なんだ。赤くもならないやつをむしって。いままでもトマトの茎をかじったりけちらしたりしたのはおまえだろう。行ってしまえ。ねこめ。」

　すると猫は肩をまるくして眼をすぼめてはいましたが口のあたりでにやにやわらって言いました。

「先生、そうお怒りになっちゃ、おからだにさわります。それよりシューマンのトロメライをひいてごらんなさい。きいてあげますから。」

「生意気なことを言うな。ねこのくせに。」

　セロ弾きはしゃくにさわって、このねこのやつどうしてくれようと、しばらく考えました。

「いやご遠慮はありません。どうぞ。わたしはどうも先生の音楽をきかないとねむられないんです。」

「生意気だ。生意気だ。生意気だ。」

　ゴーシュはすっかりまっ赤になって、ひるま楽長のし

He went on long past midnight, till in the end he hardly knew whether it was himself playing or someone else. He looked awful, as though he might collapse at any moment, his eyes all bloodshot and his face bright red.

Just then, though, somebody tapped three times on the door behind him.

"Is that you, Horsch?" he called as though half-asleep. However, it wasn't Horsch who pushed open the door and came in, but a large tortoiseshell cat that he had seen around several times before.

The cat was carrying, with enormous effort it seemed, a half-ripe tomato from Gorsch's field, which he set down in front of him.

"Phew. That was tiring," he said "Carrying things is a terrible job."

"What on earth… ?" exclaimed Gorsch.

"It's a present for you," said the tortoiseshell cat.

All the annoyance Gorsch had been damming up inside him since earlier that day came bursting out at once.

"Who told you to bring any tomato? Why should I want anything from somebody like you? And that tomato, what's more, comes from my field. What do you think you're up to?—picking them before they're ripe! I suppose it's you, then, who's been biting at the stalks and scattering them all over the place? Get out of here, you damn cat!"

All this made the visitor's shoulders droop and his eyes narrow, but he forced a grin and said, "You should-n't get so angry, sir, it's bad for your health. Why don't you play something instead? Schumann's 'Träumerei,' say…. I'll be your audience."

たように足ぶみしてどなりましたが、にわかに気を変えて言いました。

「では弾くよ。」ゴーシュはなんと思ったか扉にかぎをかって窓もみんなしめてしまい、それからセロをとりだしてあかしを消しました。すると外から二十日過ぎの月のひかりが室のなかへ半分ほどはいってきました。

「何をひけと。」

「トロメライ、ロマチックシューマン作曲。」猫は口をふいてすまして言いました。

「そうか。トロメライというのはこういうのか。」セロ弾きはなんと思ったか、まずはんけちを引きさいてじぶんの耳の穴へぎっしりつめました。それからまるで嵐のような勢いで、「印度の虎狩り」という譜を弾きはじめました。

　すると猫はしばらく首をまげて聞いていましたがいきなりパチパチパチッと眼をしたかと思うとぱっと扉の方へ飛びのきました。そしていきなりどんと扉へからだをぶっつけましたが扉はあきませんでした。猫はさあこれはもう一生一代の失敗をしたというふうにあわてだして眼や額からぱちぱち火花を出しました。するとこんどは口のひげからも鼻からも出ましたから猫はくすぐったがって、しばらくくしゃみをするような顔をして、それからさあこうしてはいられないぞというようにはせあるきだしました。ゴーシュはすっかりおもしろくなってますます勢いよくやりだしました。

「先生もうたくさんです。たくさんですよ。ご生ですからやめてください。これからもう先生のタクトなんかとりませんから。」

「だまれ。これから虎をつかまえる所だ。」

174

"I've never heard such damned impertinence. And from a cat!"

Feeling furious, Gorsch spent a while thinking of the things he'd like to do to this creature.

"Come on, don't be shy," said the cat. "Please. You know, I can't get to sleep unless I hear you play something."

"That's enough of your cheek! Enough, I say! Enough!"

Gorsch had gone an even brighter red and was shouting and stamping just as the conductor had done earlier that day. Suddenly, though, he changed his mind and said, "All right, then, I'll play!" Ominously, he locked the door and shut all the windows, then got his cello out and turned off the light. When he did so, the light of the moon shone halfway into the room from outside.

"What was it you wanted to hear?"

"… 'Träumerei.' By Schumann," said the cat in a perfectly serious voice, wiping his mouth as he spoke.

"Oh. 'Träumerei.' Of course. Would this be how it goes?"

Ominously again he tore his handkerchief into strips and stuffed up both his ears. Then he stormed straight into a piece called "Tiger Hunt in India."

For a while the cat listened with bowed head, but all of a sudden he blinked his eyes rapidly and made a leap for the door. His body collided with the door, but it refused to open. This threw the cat into a great state of agitation, and sparks crackled from his eyes and forehead. Then sparks came from his whiskers and nose too, which tickled, so that for a while he looked as if he was going to sneeze, and he started trotting around as though he couldn't stay still. Gorsch was delighted at the effect he was producing, and began to play all the harder.

猫はくるしがってはねあがってまわったり壁にからだ
をくっつけたりしましたが、壁についたあとはしばらく
青くひかるのでした。しまいは猫はまるで風車のように
ぐるぐるぐるぐるゴーシュをまわりました。ゴーシュも
すこしぐるぐるしてきましたので、
「さあこれで許してやるぞ。」と言いながらようようや
めました。
　すると猫もけろりとして、
「先生、こんやの演奏はどうかしてますね。」と言いま
した。
　セロ弾きはまたぐっとしゃくにさわりましたが何気な
いふうで巻きたばこを一本だして口にくわえ、それから
マッチを一本とって、
「どうだい。ぐあいをわるくしないかい。舌を出してご
らん。」
　猫はばかにしたようにとがった長い舌をベロリと出し
ました。
　「ははあ、少し荒れたね。」セロ弾きは言いながらい
きなりマッチを舌でシュッとすってじぶんのたばこへつ
けました。さあ猫はおどろいたのなんの、舌を風車のよ
うにふりまわしながら入り口の扉へ行って頭でどんとぶ
っつかってはよろよろとして、また戻って来てどんとぶ
っつかってはよろよろ、また戻って来てまたぶっつかっ
てはよろよろにげみちをこさえようとしました。
　ゴーシュはしばらくおもしろそうに見ていましたが、
「出してやるよ、もう来るなよ。ばか。」
　セロ弾きは扉をあけて猫が風のように萱のなかを走っ
て行くのを見てちょっとわらいました。それからやっと
せいせいしたというようにぐっすりねむりました。

"Mr. Gorsch, that's enough, thank you," said the cat. "Quite enough. I beg you to stop. I promise I'll never tell you what to do again.

"Be quiet! We're just getting to the bit where they catch the tiger."

By now the cat was leaping up and down in distress, then racing around the walls, which gave off a green glow for a while when he rubbed against them. In the end, he was whirling like a merry-go-round.

Gorsch's own head began to spin a little, so he said, "All right, I'll let you off now." And at last he stopped.

The cat forced himself to look calm. "Mr. Gorsch, there's something funny about your playing tonight, isn't there?" he said.

Again Gorsch felt deeply aggrieved but, as casually as he could, he got out a cigarette and put it in his mouth, then took a match and said, "What about it? Are you sure there's nothing wrong with *you*? Let's have a look at your tongue."

Rather rudely the cat stuck out his long, pointed tongue.

"Ah-ha! Looks a bit rough, I'm afraid," said the cellist, and without warning he struck the match on it and lit his cigarette. To say the cat was startled would be putting it too mildly: waving his tongue about like a pinwheel, he ran to the door and bashed his head against it, staggered away, went back and banged it again, staggered, went back again, banged it once more and staggered, trying desperately to escape.

For a while Gorsch watched in amusement, then said, "I'll let you out. So mind you don't come again. Stupid!"

次の晩もゴーシュがまた黒いセロの包みをかついで帰ってきました。そして水をごくごくのむとそっくりゆうべのとおりぐんぐんセロを弾きはじめました。十二時はまもなく過ぎ一時もすぎ二時もすぎてもゴーシュはまだやめませんでした。それからもう何時だかもわからず弾いているかもわからずごうごうやっていますと誰か屋根裏をこつこつとたたくものがあります。

「猫、まだこりないのか。」

　ゴーシュが叫びますと、いきなり天井の穴からぽろんと音がして一疋の灰いろの鳥が降りて来まして、床へとまったのを見るとそれはかっこうでした。

「鳥まで来るなんて。なんの用だ。」ゴーシュが言いました。

「音楽を教わりたいのです。」

　かっこう鳥はすまして言いました。

　ゴーシュは笑って、

「音楽だと。おまえの歌は、かっこう、かっこうというだけじゃあないか。」

　するとかっこうがたいへんまじめに、

「ええ、それなんです。けれどもむずかしいですからねえ。」と言いました。

「むずかしいもんか。おまえたちのはたくさん啼くのがひどいだけで、なきようはなんでもないじゃないか。」

「ところがそれがひどいんです。たとえば、かっこうとこうなくのと、かっこう　とこうなくのとでは聞いていてもよほどちがうでしょう。」

「ちがわないね。」

「ではあなたにはわからないんです。わたしらのなかまなら、かっこうと一万言えば一万みんなちがうんです。」

178

He opened the door, and the cat streaked off through the reeds. Gorsch gave a little smile as he watched him go, then went to bed and slept soundly as though a load had been lifted from his mind.

The next evening, too, Gorsch came home with the same black bundle on his back and, after gulping down a great deal of water, began to scrub away at his cello again. Soon twelve o'clock came, then one, then two, and still Gorsch went on. And he was still booming away, scarcely aware of the time or even of the fact that he was playing, when he heard someone tapping on the other side of the ceiling.

"What!... Haven't you had enough yet, Cat?" he shouted, whereupon a scuffling sound came from a hole in the ceiling and a gray bird flew down through it and landed on the floor. It was a cuckoo.

"So now I have birds, too," said Gorsch. "What do *you* want?"

"I want to learn music," said the cuckoo quite seriously.

"Music, eh?" said Gorsch with a smile. "But all you can sing is *cuckoo*, *cuckoo*, surely?"

"Yes," said the cuckoo earnestly, "that's right. But it's very difficult to do, you know."

"Difficult? The only problem for cuckoos is having to sing such a lot. There's nothing difficult about the actual notes, is there?"

"No, actually that's just why it's so hard. For example, if I sing like this—*cuckoo*—and then like this—*cuckoo*—you can tell they're different just by listening, can't you?" "They sound the same to me."

"That's because your ear's not sensitive enough. We

「かってだよ。そんなにわかってるなら何もおれの処へ来なくてもいいではないか。」
「ところが私はドレミファを正確にやりたいんです。」
「ドレミファもくそもあるか。」
「ええ、外国へ行く前にぜひ一度いるんです。」
「外国もくそもあるか。」
「先生どうかドレミファを教えてください。わたしはついてうたいますから。」
「うるさいなあ。そら三べんだけ弾いてやるから、すんだらさっさと帰るんだぞ。」
　ゴーシュはセロを取り上げてボロンボロンと糸を合わせて、ドレミファソラシドとひきました。
　するとかっこうはあわてて羽をばたばたしました。
「ちがいます、ちがいます。そんなんでないんです。」
「うるさいなあ。ではおまえやってごらん。」
「こうですよ。」かっこうはからだをまえに曲げてしばらく構えてから、
「かっこう。」と一つなきました。
「なんだい。それがドレミファかい。おまえたちには、それではドレミファも第六交響曲も同じなんだな。」
「それはちがいます。」
「どうちがうんだ。」
「むずかしいのは、これをたくさん続けたのがあるんです。」
「つまりこうだろう。」セロ弾きはまたセロをとって、かっこう　かっこう　かっこう　かっこう　かっこうとつづけてひきました。
　するとかっこうはたいへんよろこんで途中から、かっこう　かっこう　かっこう　かっこうとついて叫びまし

could sing ten thousand *cuckoo*s and to us they'd all be different."

"I'll take your word for it. If you're so good at it, though, why do you have to come to me?"

"But you see, I want to learn the scale correctly."

"Why should you care about the scale?"

"Oh, but one needs it if one's going abroad."

"And why should *you* care about going abroad?"

"Sir—please teach me the scale. I'll sing it with you as you play."

"Oh, hell! Look, I'll play it just three times, then when I've finished I want you out of here."

Gorsch took up his cello, scraped at the strings as he tuned them, then played *do, re, mi, fa, sol, la ti, do*.

But the cuckoo fluttered his wings in dismay.

"No, no. That's not how it should go."

"There's just no pleasing you. You try it, then."

"This is how it goes." The bird bent forward slightly, braced himself, and produced a single *cuckoo*.

"Well! Do you call that a scale? If it is, then an ordinary scale and the Sixth Symphony must sound all the same to you cuckoos."

"Oh no, they're quite different."

"How?"

"One of the difficult things is when you get a lot of them in succession."

"You mean like this, I suppose?" Gorsch took up his cello again and started to play a number of *cuckoo*s in succession.

This delighted the bird so much that halfway through he began to bawl *cuckoo, cuckoo*, in time with Gorsch. On and on he went, twisting his body to and fro.

た。それももう一生けん命からだをまげていつまでも叫ぶのです。

　ゴーシュはそろそろ手が痛くなって、

「こら、いいかげんにしないか。」と言いながらやめました。

　するとかっこうは残念そうに眼をつりあげて、まだしばらくないていましたがやっと、

「かっこう　かくう　かっ　かっ　かっ　か。」

　といってやめました。

　ゴーシュがすっかりおこってしまって、

「こら、とり、もう用が済んだらかえれ。」と言いました。

「どうかもういっぺん弾いてください。あなたのはいいようだけれどもすこしちがうんです。」

「なんだと、おれがきさまに教わってるんではないんだぞ。帰らんか。」

「どうか、たったもう一ぺんおねがいです。どうか。」

　かっこうは頭を何べんもてんてん下げました。

「ではこれっきりだよ。」

　ゴーシュは弓をかまえました。かっこうは、

「くっ。」とひとつ息をして、

「ではなるべく永くおねがいいたします。」といってまた一つおじぎをしました。

「いやになっちまうなあ。」ゴーシュはにが笑いしながら弾きはじめました。するとかっこうはまたまるで本気になって、

「かっこう　かっこう　かっこう。」とからだをまげてじつに一生けん命叫びました。

　ゴーシュははじめはむしゃくしゃしていましたが、いつまでもつづけて弾いているうちにふっとなんだかこれ

Eventually Gorsch's hand began to hurt, so he stopped.

"Here," he said, "that's about enough, isn't it?"

But the cuckoo just narrowed his eyes regretfully and went on singing for a while, till finally he went *cuckoo, cuck—cuck—cuck—cu*—and stopped. By now Gorsch was getting angry. "Look—if you've finished, you can clear out." "Oh, please. Won't you play it just once more? There's something still not quite right about your side of it." "What? I'm not supposed to be learning from you. Come on, go home."

"Please, just one more time. Please…," said the bird, humbly bobbing his head.

"Well, then, just this once." Gorsch got his bow ready.

The cuckoo gave a single *cuck!* then said, "As long as possible if you don't mind." He bowed his head again.

"Heaven help us," said Gorsch, and with a wry smile began to play. Again the cuckoo got quite wrapped up in things and sang for all he was worth, twisting back and forth: *cuckoo, cuckoo, cuckoo*.

At first Gorsch felt very irritated, but as he played on he began to have an odd feeling that it was the cuckoo, somehow, who was really hitting the notes of the scale. In fact, the more he played the more convinced he became that the cuckoo was better than he was.

"Hell! I'll go cuckoo myself if I keep this up," he said, and quite abruptly stopped.

The bird reeled as though someone had banged him on the head, then, just as he'd done before, sang *cuckoo, cuckoo, cuck—cuck—cuck*—and stopped.

"Why did you stop?" the bird said, looking at Gorsch resentfully. "Any cuckoo worth his salt would've kept on

は鳥の方がほんとうのドレミファにはまっているかなという気がしてきました。

　どうも弾けば弾くほどかっこうの方がいいような気がするのでした。

「えいこんなばかなことしていたらおれは鳥になってしまうんじゃないか。」

　とゴーシュはいきなりぴたりとセロをやめました。

　するとかっこうはどしんと頭をたたかれたようにふらふらっとして、それからまたさっきのように、

「かっこう　かっこう　かっこう　かっ　かっ　かっ　かっ　かっ。」と言ってやめました。それから恨めしそうに、ゴーシュを見て、

「なぜやめたんですか。ぼくらならどんないくじないやつでも、のどから血が出るまでは叫ぶんですよ。」と言いました。

「何を生意気な。こんなばかなまねをいつまでしていられるか。もう出て行け。見ろ。夜があけるんじゃないか。」ゴーシュは窓を指さしました。

　東のそらがぽうっと銀いろになって、そこをまっ黒な雲が北の方へどんどん走っています。

「ではお日さまの出るまでどうぞ。もう一ぺん。ちょっとですから。」

　かっこうはまた頭を下げました。

「黙れっ。いい気になって。このばか鳥め。出て行かんとむしって朝飯に食ってしまうぞ。」

　ゴーシュはどんと床をふみました。

　するとかっこうはにわかにびっくりしたように、いきなり窓をめがけて飛び立ちました。そして硝子にはげしく頭をぶっつけてばたっと下へ落ちました。

「なんだ、硝子へ、ばかだなあ。」ゴーシュはあわてて

singing at the top of his voice till his throat was too sore to go on."

"Why, you cheeky... Do you think I can go on fooling around like this forever? Come on, now, get out. Look—can't you see it's nearly dawn?" He pointed at the window.

The eastern sky was turning faintly silver where black clouds were scudding across it toward the north. "Couldn't we just go on till it's light? It's only a little while to wait."

Again the cuckoo bowed his head.

"That's enough! You seem to think you can get away with anything. If you don't get out I'll pluck your feathers and eat you for breakfast, you stupid bird." He stamped hard on the floor. This seemed to frighten the cuckoo, for suddenly he flew up toward the window, only to bang his head violently against the glass and flop down on the floor again.

"Look at you, you fool—banging into the glass!" Hastily Gorsch got up to open the window, but the window never had been the kind to slide open at a touch, and he was still rattling the frame furiously when the cuckoo slammed into it and fell again.

Gorsch could see a little blood coming from the base of his beak.

"I'm going to open it for you, so wait a moment, won't you?" With great difficulty he had just got the thing open a couple of inches when the cuckoo picked himself up and, staring hard at the eastern sky beyond the window as though he was determined to succeed at all costs this time, took off with frantically beating wings. This time, of course, he hit the window even

立って窓をあけようとしましたが、元来この窓はそんなにいつでもするする開く窓ではありませんでした。ゴーシュが窓のわくをしきりにがたがたしているうちに、またかっこうがぱっとぶっつかって下へ落ちました。

　見ると嘴のつけねからすこし血が出ています。

「いまあけてやるから待っていろったら。」ゴーシュがやっと二寸ばかり窓をあけたとき、かっこうは起きあがって何がなんでもこんどこそというようにじっと窓の向こうの東のそらをみつめて、あらん限りの力をこめたふうでぱっと飛びたちました。もちろんこんどは前よりひどく硝子につきあたってかっこうは下へ落ちたまましばらく身動きもしませんでした。つかまえてドアから飛ばしてやろうとゴーシュが手を出しましたら、いきなりかっこうは眼をひらいて飛びのきました。そしてまたガラスへ飛びつきそうにするのです。ゴーシュは思わず足を上げて窓をばっとけりました。ガラスは二、三枚ものすごい音して砕け窓はわくのまま外へ落ちました。そのがらんとなった窓のあとをかっこうが矢のように外へ飛びだしました。そしてもうどこまでもどこまでもまっすぐに飛んで行って、とうとう見えなくなってしまいました。ゴーシュはしばらくあきれたように外を見ていましたが、そのまま倒れるように室のすみへころがってねむってしまいました。

　次の晩もゴーシュは夜中すぎまでセロを弾いてつかれて水を一杯のんでいますと、また扉をこつこつとたたくものがあります。

　今夜は何が来てもゆうべのかっこうのようにはじめからおどかして追い払ってやろうと思ってコップをもったまま待ち構えておりますと、扉がすこしあいて一疋の狸の子がはいってきました。

186

more violently than before and dropped to the floor, where he remained perfectly still for a while. But when Gorsch put a hand out, thinking to take him to the door and let him fly away, the bird suddenly opened his eyes and leapt out of reach. It looked as though he was going to fly into the window again, so, almost without thinking, Gorsch raised his leg and gave the window a great kick.

Two or three panes shattered with a tremendous crash and the whole thing fell outside, frame and all. Through the gaping hole it left the cuckoo flew out like an arrow. On and on he flew into the distance till finally he completely disappeared from sight. For a while Gorsch stayed looking out in disgust, then flopped down in a corner of the room and went to sleep where he was.

The next day, too, Gorsch played his cello until past midnight. He was tired and was drinking a glass of water when again there came a tapping at the door.

Whoever his visitor might be, he told himself, he would take a threatening attitude from the start and drive him away before the same thing happened as with the cuckoo. As he waited with the glass in his hand, the door opened a little and a badger cub came in. Gorsch opened the door a bit wider, then stamped on the floor.

"Listen, you," he shouted, "do you know what badger soup is?" But the badger seated himself tidily on the floor with a puzzled look on his face and sat thinking for a while, his head tilted to one side. "Badger soup?" said the badger in a little voice. "No." The look on the cub's face made Gorsch want to burst out laughing, but he put on a fierce expression and went on: "Then I'll tell you.

ゴーシュはそこでその扉をもう少し広くひらいておいてどんと足をふんで、

「こら、狸、おまえは狸汁ということを知っているかっ。」

とどなりました。すると狸の子はぼんやりした顔をしてきちんと床へすわったまま、どうもわからないというように首をまげて考えていましたが、しばらくたって、

「狸汁ってぼく知らない。」と言いました。ゴーシュはその顔を見て思わず吹き出そうとしましたが、まだ無理にこわい顔をして、

「では教えてやろう。狸汁というのはな。おまえのような狸を、キャベジや塩とまぜてくたくたと煮ておれさまの食うようにしたものだ。」と言いました。すると狸の子はまたふしぎそうに、

「だってぼくのお父さんがね、ゴーシュさんはとてもいい人でこわくないから行って習えと言ったよ。」と言いました。そこでゴーシュもとうとう笑いだしてしまいました。

「何を習えと言ったんだ。おれはいそがしいんじゃないか。それにねむいんだよ。」

　狸の子はにわかに勢いがついたように一足前へ出ました。

「ぼくは小太鼓の係りでねえ。セロへ合わせてもらって来いと言われたんだ。」

「どこにも小太鼓がないじゃないか。」

「そら、これ。」狸の子はせなかから棒きれを二本出しました。

「それでどうするんだ。」

「ではね、『愉快な馬車屋』を弾いてください。」

「なんだ愉快な馬車屋ってジャズか。」

「ああ、この譜だよ。」狸の子はせなかからまた一枚の譜をとり出しました。ゴーシュは手にとってわらいだしました。

Badger soup, you see, is a badger just like you boiled up with cabbage and salt for the likes of me to eat."

The young badger still looked puzzled and said, "But my father, you know, he said I was to go and study with Mr. Gorsch because he was a very nice man and not at all to be scared of."

At this, Gorsch finally laughed out loud. "What did he tell you to study?" he said. "I'm busy, I'll have you know. And I'm sleepy, too."

The little badger stepped forward as though he had suddenly taken heart.

"You see, I'm the one who plays the side drum," he said, "and I was told to go and learn how to play in time with the cello." "But I don't see any side drum."

"Here—look." The badger produced two sticks that were slung across his back.

"And what are you going to do with those?"

"Play 'The Happy Coachman,' please, and you'll see."

"'The Happy Coachman'? What's that—jazz or something?"

"Here's the music."

This time the badger brought out from behind his back a single sheet of music. Gorsch took it from him and laughed.

"Well, this is a funny piece of music! All right. Here we go, then. So you're going to play the drum, are you?" And he started playing, watching the cub out of the corner of his eye to see what he would do.

To Gorsch's surprise, the badger started busily beating with his sticks on the body of the cello below the bridge. He was not at all bad at it, and, as he played, Gorsch found himself beginning to enjoy things.

「ふう、変な曲だなあ。よし、さあ弾くぞ。おまえは小太鼓をたたくのか。」ゴーシュは狸の子がどうするのかと思ってちらちらそっちを見ながら弾きはじめました。

するとうと狸の子は棒をもってセロの駒の下のところを拍子をとってぽんぽんたたきはじめました。それがなかなかうまいので弾いているうちにゴーシュはこれはおもしろいぞと思いました。

おしまいまでひいてしまうと狸の子はしばらく首をまげて考えました。

それからやっと考えついたというように言いました。「ゴーシュさんはこの二番目の糸をひくときはきたいに遅れるねえ。なんだかぼくがつまずくようになるよ。」

ゴーシュははっとしました。たしかにその糸はどんなに手早く弾いてもすこしたってからでないと音が出ないような気がゆうべからしていたのでした。

「いや、そうかもしれない。このセロは悪いんだよ。」とゴーシュはかなしそうに言いました。すると狸はきのどくそうにして、またしばらく考えていましたが、

「どこが悪いんだろうなあ。ではもう一ぺん弾いてくれますか。」

「いいとも弾くよ。」ゴーシュははじめました。狸の子はさっきのようにとんとんたたきながら時々頭をまげてセロに耳をつけるようにしました。そしておしまいまで来たときは今夜もまた東がぼうと明るくなっていました。

「ああ夜が明けたぞ。どうもありがとう。」狸の子はたいへんあわてて譜や棒きれをせなかへしょってゴムテープでぱちんととめておじぎを二つ三つすると急いで外へ出て行ってしまいました。

ゴーシュはぼんやりしてしばらくゆうべのこわれたガ

When they got to the end, the badger stayed thinking for a while with his head on one side. At last he seemed to reach a conclusion of some kind, for he said, "When you play this second string you get behind, don't you? Somehow it seems to throw me off the beat."

Gorsch was taken aback. It was true: ever since yesterday evening he'd had a feeling that however smartly he played that particular string, there was always a pause before it sounded.

"You know, you may be right. This cello's no good," he said sadly. The badger looked sympathetic and thought again for a while.

"I wonder where it's no good. Would you mind playing it once more?"

"Of course." Gorsch started up again. The badger beat away as before, tilting his head to one side occasionally as though listening to the cello. And by the time they had finished there was a glimmering of light again in the east.

"Look—it's getting near dawn. Thank you very much." Hastily the little badger hoisted the sticks and the music onto his back, fastened them there with a rubber band, gave two or three bows, and hurried out of the house.

For a while Gorsch sat there abstractedly, breathing in the cool air that came through the windowpanes he'd broken the previous night, then decided to go to sleep and get his strength back for going into town, and crawled into bed.

The next day, too, Gorsch was up all night playing his cello. It was almost dawn, and he had begun to doze

ラスからはいってくる風を吸っていましたが、町へ出て
行くまでねむって元気をとり戻そうと急いでねどこへも
ぐり込みました。

　次の晩もゴーシュは夜通しセロを弾いて明け方近く思
わずつかれて楽譜をもったまま、うとうとしていますと、
また誰か扉をこつこつとたたくものがあります。それも
まるで聞こえるか聞こえないかのくらいでしたが毎晩の
ことなのでゴーシュはすぐ聞きつけて、

「おはいり。」と言いました。すると戸のすきまからは
いって来たのは一ぴきの野ねずみでした。そしてたいへ
んちいさなこどもをつれてちょろちょろとゴーシュの前
へ歩いてきました。

　そのまた野ねずみのこどもときたら、まるでけしごむ
のくらいしかないのでゴーシュはおもわず笑いました。
すると野ねずみは何をわらわれたろうというようにきょ
ろきょろしながら青い栗の実を一つぶ前においてちゃん
とおじぎをして言いました。

「先生、この児があんばいがわるくて死にそうでござい
ます。先生どうぞお慈悲になおしてやってくださいま
し。」

「おれが医者などやれるもんか。」ゴーシュはすこしむ
っとして言いました。すると野ねずみのお母さんは下を
向いてしばらくだまっていましたがまた思い切ったよう
に言いました。

「先生、それはうそでございます。先生はあんなにじょ
うずにみんなの病気をなおしておいでになるではありま
せんか。」

「なんのことだかわからんね。」

「だって先生、先生のおかげで、兎さんのおばあさんも

off with the score still held in his hand, when again he heard someone tapping. It was so faint that it was hard to be sure whether somebody had really knocked or not, but Gorsch, who was used to it by now, heard at once and said, "Come in."

The door opened an inch or two, and in came a field mouse leading an extremely small child mouse. Hesitantly, she came toward Gorsch. As for the baby mouse, it was so small—only about as big as an eraser— that Gorsch couldn't help smiling. Peering about her as though wondering what he could be smiling at, the mother set down a green chestnut in front of her and bowed very correctly.

"Mr. Gorsch," she said. "This child here isn't well, and I'm afraid he may die. I beg you, out of the kindness of your heart, to cure him."

"How can you expect *me* to do that?" demanded Gorsch rather petulantly.

The mother mouse looked down at the floor and was silent for a while, then seemed to pluck up courage and said, "I know very well that you cure all kinds of people every day, and that you're very good at it, too." "I don't know what you're talking about." "But it was thanks to you that the rabbit's grandmother got better, wasn't it, and the badger's father, and even that nasty old owl was cured, wasn't he, so in the circumstances I think it's very unkind of you to say you won't save this child."

"Wait a minute—there must be some mistake. *I've* never cured any sick owl. Though it's true I had the young badger here last night, behaving like a member of the band." He laughed, looking down at the baby mouse in dismay. But the mother mouse started crying.

なおりましたし、狸さんのお父さんもなおりましたし、あんないじわるのみみずくまでなおしていただいたのに、この子ばかりお助けをいただけないとはあんまり情けないことでございます。」

「おいおい、それは何かのまちがいだよ。おれはみみずくの病気なんどなおしてやったことはないからな。もっとも狸の子はゆうべ来て楽隊のまねをして行ったがね。ははん。」

ゴーシュはあきれてその子ねずみを見おろしてわらいました。

すると野鼠のお母さんは泣きだしてしまいました。

「ああこの児はどうせ病気になるならもっと早くなればよかった。さっきまであれくらいごうごうと鳴らしておいでになったのに、病気になるといっしょにぴたっと音がとまって、もうあとはいくらおねがいしても鳴らしてくださらないなんて。なんてふしあわせな子どもだろう。」

ゴーシュはびっくりして叫びました。

「なんだと、ぼくがセロを弾けばみみずくや兎の病気がなおると。どういうわけだ。それは。」

野ねずみは眼を片手でこすりこすり言いました。

「はい、ここらのものは病気になるとみんな先生のおうちの床下にはいって療すのでございます。」

「すると療るのか。」

「はい。からだじゅうとても血のまわりがよくなってたいへんいい気持ちですぐに療るかたもあれば、うちへ帰ってから療るかたもあります。」

「ああそうか。おれのセロの音がごうごうひびくと、それがあんまの代わりになっておまえたちの病気がなおるというのか。よし。わかったよ。やってやろう。」ゴーシュはちょっとギュウギュウと糸を合わせて、それから

"Ah me, if the child *had* to get sick I only wish he'd done it sooner. There you were rumbling away here just a while ago, then as soon as he gets sick the sound stops dead and you refuse to play any more. The poor little thing."

"What?" shouted Gorsch, startled. "You mean that when I play, sick rabbits and owls get better? Why, I wonder?"

"You see," said the field mouse, rubbing at her eyes with a paw, "whenever the folk around here get sick, they creep under the floor of your house." "And you mean they get well?"

"Yes, it improves the circulation wonderfully. They feel so much better. Some of them are cured on the spot, others after they're back home again."

"Ah, I see. You mean that when my cello rumbles it acts as a kind of massage?... Now I understand. All right, I'll play for you."

いきなりねずみのこどもをつまんでセロの孔から中へ入れてしまいました。

「わたしもいっしょについて行きます。どこの病院でもそうですから。」

おっかさんの野ねずみはきちがいのようになってセロに飛びつきました。

「おまえさんもはいるかね。」

セロ弾きはおっかさんの野ねずみをセロの孔からくぐらしてやろうとしましたが顔が半分しかはいりませんでした。

野ねずみはばたばたしながら中のこどもに叫びました。

「おまえそこはいいかい。落ちるときいつも教えるように足をそろえてうまく落ちたかい。」

「いい。うまく落ちた。」こどものねずみはまるで蚊のような小さな声でセロの底で返事しました。

「大丈夫さ。だから泣き声出すなというんだ。」

ゴーシュはおっかさんのねずみを下におろして、それから弓をとってなんとかラプソディとかいうものをごうごうがあがあ弾きました。するとおっかさんねずみはいかにも心配そうにその音のぐあいをきいていましたがとうとうこらえきれなくなったふうで、

「もうたくさんです。どうか出してやってください。」

と言いました。

「なあんだ、これでいいのか。」ゴーシュはセロをまげて孔のところに手をあてて待っていましたらまもなくこどものねずみが出てきました。ゴーシュはだまってそれをおろしてやりました。見るとすっかり目をつぶってぶるぶるぶるぶるふるえていました。

「どうだったの。いいかい。気分は。」

He squeaked at the strings a bit to tune them, then all of a sudden picked up the baby mouse between his fingers and popped him in through the hole in the cello.

"I'll go with him," said the mother mouse frantically, jumping onto the cello. "All the hospitals allow it"

"So you're going in as well, eh?" said Gorsch, and tried to help her through the hole, but she could only get her face halfway in.

"Are you all right there?" she called to the child inside as she pushed and struggled. "Did you fall properly as I always tell you you should, with your paws foursquare?"

"I'm all right. I fell nicely," came the baby mouse's voice from the bottom of the cello, so faint it could hardly be heard.

"Of course he's all right," said Gorsch. "So we don't want you crying, now.

Gorsch set the mother down on the floor, then took up his bow and rumbled and scraped his way through some rhapsody or other. The mother sat listening anxiously to the quality of the sound, but finally, it seemed, she could bear the suspense no longer and said, "That's enough, thank you. Could you take him out now, please?"

"Well! Is that all?" Gorsch tipped the cello over, put his hand by the hole, and waited. Almost immediately, the baby mouse appeared. Without saying anything, Gorsch set him down on the floor. The baby's eyes were shut tight and he was trembling and trembling as though he would never stop.

"How was it? How do you feel? Better?" asked the mother mouse.

こどものねずみはすこしもへんじもしないで、まだしばらく眼をつぶったままぶるぶるぶるぶるふるえていましたが、にわかに起き上がって走りだしました。

「ああ、よくなったんだ。ありがとうございます。ありがとうございます。」おっかさんのねずみもいっしょに走っていましたが、まもなくゴーシュの前に来てしきりにおじぎをしながら、「ありがとうございます、ありがとうございます。」と十ばかり言いました。

　ゴーシュはなんだかかあいそうになって、

「おい、おまえたちはパンはたべるのか。」とききました。すると野鼠がびっくりしたようにきょろきょろあたりを見まわしてから、

「いえ、もうおパンというものは小麦の粉をこねたりおしたりしてこしらえたもので、ふくふくふくらんでいておいしいものなそうでございますが、そうでなくても私どもはおうちの戸棚へなど参ったこともございませんし、ましてこれくらいお世話になりながらどうしてそれを運びになんど参れましょう。」

　と言いました。

「いや、そのことではないんだ。ただたべるのかときいたんだ。ではたべるんだな。ちょっと待てよ。その腹の悪いこどもへやるからな。」

　ゴーシュはセロを床へ置いて戸棚からパンを一つまみむしって野ねずみの前へ置きました。

　野ねずみはもうまるでばかのようになって泣いたり笑ったりおじぎをしたりしてから大じそうにそれをくわえてこどもをさきに立て、外へ出て行きました。

「あああ。鼠と話するのもなかなかつかれるぞ。」ゴーシュはねどこへどっかり倒れてすぐぐうぐうねむってしまいました。

The child mouse made no reply but sat for a while with his eyes shut, trembling and trembling, then quite suddenly jumped up and started running about.

"Look, he's better! Thank you so much, sir, thank you so much." The mother mouse went and ran about a little with her child, but soon came back to Gorsch and, bowing busily over and over again, said, "Thank you so much, thank you so much," about ten times in all.

Somehow Gorsch felt rather sorry for them.

"Here—" he said, "do you eat bread?"

The field mouse looked shocked. "Oh, no!" she said, looking about her uneasily as she spoke. "People do say that bread is very light and good to eat—it seems they make it by kneading flour—but of course we've never been near your cupboard, and we'd never dream of coming to steal it after everything you've done for us."

"No—that's not what I mean. I'm just asking if you can eat it. But of *course* you can. Wait a moment, then, I'll give some to this boy for his bad stomach."

He set the cello down on the floor, went to the cupboard, tore off a handful of bread, and put it in front of them.

The field mouse cried and laughed and bowed as though she had gone quite silly, then with infinite care took the bread in her mouth and went out, shooing the child in front of her.

"Dear me," said Gorsch. "It's quite tiring talking to mice." And, flopping down on his bed, he was soon fast asleep and snoring.

It was the evening of the sixth day after this. With flushed faces the members of the Venus Orchestra, each

それから六日目の晩でした。金星音楽団の人たちは町の公会堂のホールの裏にある控え室へみんなぱっと顔をほてらしてめいめい楽器をもって、ぞろぞろホールの舞台から引きあげて来ました。首尾よく第六交響曲を仕上げたのです。ホールでは拍手の音がまだ嵐のように鳴っております。楽長はポケットへ手をつっ込んで拍手なんかどうでもいいというようにのそのそみんなの間を歩きまわっていましたが、じつはどうしてうれしさでいっぱいなのでした。みんなはたばこをくわえてマッチをすったり楽器をケースへ入れたりしました。

ホールはまだぱちぱち手が鳴っています。それどころではなくいよいよそれが高くなってなんだかこわいような手がつけられないような音になりました。大きな白いリボンを胸につけた司会者がはいって来ました。

「アンコールをやっていますが、何かみじかいものでもきかせてやってくださいませんか。」

すると楽長がきっとなって答えました。

「いけませんな。こういう大物のあとへ何を出したってこっちの気の済むようには行くもんでないんです。」

「では楽長さん出てちょっとあいさつしてください。」

「ためだ。おい、ゴーシュ君、何か出て弾いてやってくれ。」

「わたしがですか。」ゴーシュはあっけにとられました。

「君だ、君だ。」ヴァイオリンの一番の人がいきなり顔をあげて言いました。

「さあ出て行きたまえ。」楽長が言いました。

みんなもセロをむりにゴーシュに持たせて扉をあけるといきなり舞台へゴーシュを押し出してしまいました。ゴーシュがその孔のあいたセロをもってじつに困ってしまって舞台へ出るとみんなはそら見ろというようにいっそうひど

carrying his instrument in his hand, came straggling from the stage of the town hall to the musicians' room at the back. They had just performed the Sixth Symphony with great success. In the hall, the storm of applause was still continuing. The conductor, his hands thrust in his pockets, was slowly pacing about among them as though applause meant absolutely nothing to him, but in fact he was thoroughly delighted. Some of them were putting cigarettes between their lips and striking matches, some putting their instruments away in their cases.

The clapping was still going on in the hall. In fact, it was getting steadily louder and was beginning to sound alarmingly as though it might get out of hand. At this point, the master of ceremonies, who had a large white rosette pinned on his chest, came in.

"They're calling for an encore," he said. "Do you think you could play something short for them?"

"Afraid not," replied the conductor stiffly. "There's nothing we could do to our own satisfaction after such a major work."

"Then won't you go out and say a word to them?"

"No. Hey, Gorsch. Go and play something for them, will you?"

"Me?" said Gorsch, thoroughly taken aback.

"You—yes, you," said the concertmaster abruptly, raising his head.

"Come on, now. On you go," said the conductor.

The others thrust his cello into his hands, opened the door, and gave him a shove. As he appeared on stage holding the cello, beside himself with embarrassment, everybody clapped still more loudly as though to say, "There, you see?" Some people even seemed to be cheering.

く手をたたきました。わあと叫んだものもあるようでした。
「どこまで人をばかにするんだ。よし見ていろ。印度の虎狩りをひいてやるから。」
　ゴーシュはすっかり落ちついて舞台のまん中へ出ました。それからあの猫の来たときのようにまるで怒った象のような勢いで虎狩りを弾きました。ところが聴衆はしいんとなって一生けん命聞いています。ゴーシュはどんどん弾きました。猫がせつながってぱちぱち火花を出したところも過ぎました。扉へからだを何べんもぶっつけた所も過ぎました。
　曲が終わるとゴーシュはもうみんなの方など見もせず、ちょうどその猫のようにすばやくセロをもって楽屋へにげ込みました。すると楽屋では楽長はじめ仲間がみんな火事にでもあったあとのように眼をじっとしてひっそりすわり込んでいます。
　ゴーシュはやぶれかぶれだと思ってみんなの間をさっさとあるいて行って向こうの長椅子へどっかりとからだをおろして足を組んですわりました。
　するとみんなが一ぺんに顔をこっちへ向けてゴーシュを見ましたが、やはりまじめでべつにわらっているようでもありませんでした。
「こんやは変な晩だなあ。」
　ゴーシュは思いました。ところが楽長は立って言いました。
「ゴーシュ君、よかったぞお。あんな曲だけれどもここではみんなかなり本気になって聞いてたぞ。一週間か十日の間にずいぶん仕上げたなあ。十日前とくらべたらまるで赤ん坊と兵隊だ。やろうと思えばいつでもやれたんじゃないか、君。」
　仲間もみんな立って来て、

"Just how much fun do they think they can make of a fellow?" thought Gorsch. "Right—I'll show 'em. I'll play them 'Tiger Hunt in India.'"

Quite calmly now, he went out into the middle of the stage. And he played "Tiger Hunt" with all the energy of an angry elephant, just as he'd done the time the cat had come. A hush fell over the audience, and they listened for all they were worth. Gorsch plowed steadily on. The part where the cat had given off sparks of distress came and went. The part where he had thrown himself again and again against the door also came and went.

When the work finally came to an end, Gorsch gave not so much as a glance at the audience, but, taking up his cello, made a bolt for it, just as the cat had done, and took refuge in the musicians' room. But there he found the conductor and all his other colleagues sitting quite silent, gazing straight in front of them as though there had just been a fire.

No longer caring what happened, Gorsch walked briskly past them, plumped himself on a sofa at the other side of the room, and crossed his legs.

They all turned to look at him, but far from laughing at him, their expressions were serious.

"There's something funny about this evening," Gorsch thought to himself. But the conductor stood up and said, "Gorsch, you were wonderful! The music may not be anything much, but you kept us listening. You've improved a lot during the past week or ten days. Why, comparing it with ten days ago is like comparing a green recruit with an old campaigner. I always knew you could if you tried, Gorsch!"

「よかったぜ。」とゴーシュに言いました。

「いや、からだが丈夫だからこんなこともできるよ。普通の人なら死んでしまうからな。」楽長が向こうで言っていました。

　その晩おそくゴーシュは自分のうちへ帰って来ました。

　そしてまた水をがぶがぶのみました。それから窓をあけて、いつかかっこうの飛んで行ったと思った遠くの空をながめながら、

「ああかっこう。あのときはすまなかったなあ。おれは怒ったんじゃなかったんだ。」と言いました。

The others, too, came over to him and said, "Well done!"

"You see," the conductor was saying in the background, "he can do it because he's tough. It would kill any ordinary man."

Late that night, Gorsch went back home.

First, he had a good drink of water. Then he opened the window and, looking into the distant sky in the direction where he felt the cuckoo had gone, he said, "You know, cuckoo—I'm sorry about what happened. I wasn't really angry with you!"

ベスト・オブ 宮沢賢治短編集
みやざわけん じ たんぺんしゅう
The Tales of Miyazawa Kenji

1996年 4 月19日　　第 1 刷発行
2000年11月22日　　第10刷発行

著　者　　宮沢賢治
みやざわけん じ

翻訳者　　ジョン・ベスター

発行者　　野間佐和子

発行所　　講談社インターナショナル株式会社
　　　　　〒112-8652　東京都文京区音羽1-17-14
　　　　　電話：03-3944-6493（編集部）
　　　　　　　　 03-3944-6492（業務部・営業部）

印刷所　　大日本印刷株式会社

製本所　　大日本印刷株式会社

落丁本、乱丁本は、講談社インターナショナル業務部宛にお送りください。送
料小社負担にてお取替えいたします。なお、この本についてのお問い合わせは、
編集部宛にお願いいたします。本書の無断複写（コピー）は著作権法上での例外
を除き、禁じられています。

定価はカバーに表示してあります。

講談社バイリンガル・ブックス （オン・カセット/オンCD） 英語で聞いても面白い!

📼 印のタイトルは、英文テキスト部分を録音したカセット・テープが、また 🎵 印のタイトルは英文テキスト部分を録音したCDが発売されています。本との併用により聞く力・話す力を高め、実用的な英語が身につく格好のリスニング教材です。